King Arthur's Mouse

Tony Langham

For
Jordan and Max,
new dreamers

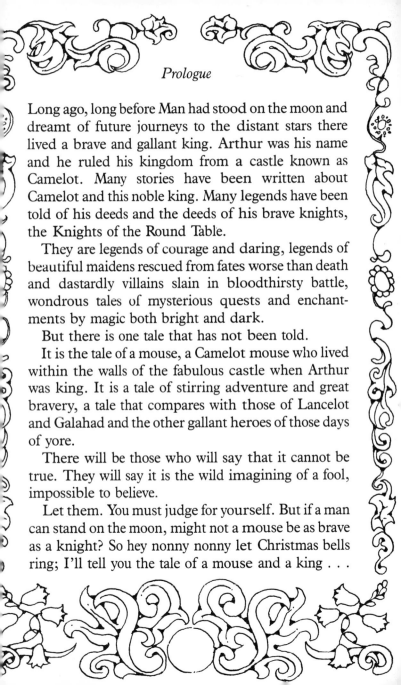

Prologue

Long ago, long before Man had stood on the moon and dreamt of future journeys to the distant stars there lived a brave and gallant king. Arthur was his name and he ruled his kingdom from a castle known as Camelot. Many stories have been written about Camelot and this noble king. Many legends have been told of his deeds and the deeds of his brave knights, the Knights of the Round Table.

They are legends of courage and daring, legends of beautiful maidens rescued from fates worse than death and dastardly villains slain in bloodthirsty battle, wondrous tales of mysterious quests and enchantments by magic both bright and dark.

But there is one tale that has not been told.

It is the tale of a mouse, a Camelot mouse who lived within the walls of the fabulous castle when Arthur was king. It is a tale of stirring adventure and great bravery, a tale that compares with those of Lancelot and Galahad and the other gallant heroes of those days of yore.

There will be those who will say that it cannot be true. They will say it is the wild imagining of a fool, impossible to believe.

Let them. You must judge for yourself. But if a man can stand on the moon, might not a mouse be as brave as a knight? So hey nonny nonny let Christmas bells ring; I'll tell you the tale of a mouse and a king . . .

Morgana le Fay stood at the window of her chamber and watched the latest guests arrive in the courtyard below. All morning the guests had been arriving. Each time the herald on the battlements blew on his trumpet it was to announce a new arrival. Lords with their ladies, knights with their squires, an endless procession of people and horses and glorious banners flying brightly in the morning light.

It was Christmas Eve at Camelot and King Arthur had ordered a great feast to be prepared in celebration. Hundreds of guests had been invited from all over the kingdom and the day was rich with the promise of a glittering occasion to come. Everybody in Camelot was excited.

Everybody except Morgana.

Morgana hated Christmas. She hated all joyful occasions. She hated everything that was bright and beautiful in life – the laughter of children, glowing sunsets, sweet-smelling flowers, the glory of colours on butterfly wings, blue skies, music, rainbows – anything and everything which ordinary people delighted in, Morgana despised.

Her midnight heart stirred to anger when people around her were happy. Had she possessed the deep magic of Merlin, the Wizard of Camelot and wise counsellor to Arthur, she would have commanded a gigantic paintbrush to paint the world black. Black was Morgana's favourite colour. Morgana wore gowns

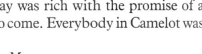

of the finest black satins and silks. Morgana wore jewels of deepest jet. Morgana rode a snorting coal-black stallion and black candles burned in her chamber at night whilst beneath black sheets and furs she dreamt her dark dreams.

And it was the dreams of Morgana which were the darkest of all, the blackest of all her blacknesses. Morgana dreamt of only one thing. She dreamt that one day she would be queen. Queen of Camelot and the kingdom which Arthur, her step-brother, now ruled. In the depths of her dreams she dreamt nightly of that triumphant moment when she ascended the throne and the royal crown was placed on her head. Only one thing stood in her way and that was Arthur himself!

How she hated him! He was everything that she was not. Arthur was loved by the people. Guided by Merlin since boyhood he ruled his kingdom justly. Rich or poor, the people knew they could rely upon him for justice. Wrongdoers who broke the king's laws were swiftly dealt with. Whenever there was a wrong to be righted he would send forth his gallant knights from Camelot. In their bright armour, on swift chargers they would ride to the aid of those who were oppressed or downtrodden, journeying far and wide to fight the forces of darkness and evil. Brave men they were, brave and chivalrous. Minstrels sang of their gallantry and mothers told their children stories of their shining adventures. They were the fairest flowers of knighthood, the pride of Camelot.

But there was one whose allegiance to Arthur was false. Modred was his name. He was a treacherous knave who hid behind a mask of loyalty, a knight whose heart was as dark as Morgana's and whose ambition for power burned equally as brightly.

Modred and Morgana. Twin evils of intent.

For months now they had plotted to end Arthur's reign. Together, secretly, whilst the rest of Camelot slept they wove their dreams of death for the king. Nothing less would do! Arthur must die and die he would! It had all been a question of waiting for the right moment and, at last, that moment now approached. What better time would there be to perform the dreadful deed? That night, Camelot would be bursting at the seams. Who would not admit that amongst the invited guests there might be one who wished the king dead? Even the noblest of kings had enemies. What an opportunity to strike and how sweet it was, Morgana thought, as she watched more honoured guests arrive, that Arthur should be the one to provide it for them. How sweet, that on this night of joy brave Arthur would forfeit his life. Fools! Morgana thought as she watched. You think you come to celebrate with Arthur, not knowing that to his funeral you come!

It was almost too much for Morgana to bear. She danced away from the window and around her chamber. She was delirious with dark joy. "Queen Morgana," she trilled, "Morgana the queen. Arthur shall die and Morgana be queen!"

Something dark and furry stirred on her bed, disturbed by the dreadful song. Morgana scooped it up in her arms as she danced by.

"Well, Wolfbane my pet, what do you think? Shall I make a good queen?"

7

Wolfbane, Morgana's gigantic cat, yawned and stretched himself. He was as black as a raven's wing and as sleek. Wolfbane purred contentedly as his mistress stroked him.

"What's that you say?" Morgana asked, "I shall do splendidly. Thank you my precious." She hugged the creature and then threw him quite gently back onto the bed where he settled and curled himself around himself once again.

High on the battlements the trumpeter unleashed another welcome. Morgana returned to the window.

Into the courtyard galloped a group of riders. It was Arthur himself returning from a hunt with some of his knights. They were laughing and joking together. It had been a good hunt. Two huge, hairy, wild boars hung from poles carried by servants who followed behind. The boars would be part of the fine fare which Arthur would offer his guests that night. Morgana smiled cruelly. A fitting meat for a funeral feast.

She watched the brightly-dressed figures pass into the Great Hall entrance, opposite her chamber. As they disappeared from sight it began to snow. The sky above the towers of Camelot was as white as a Sunday petticoat. Morgana watched as the flakes floated slowly past her window. She held out her hand and some of the flakes settled softly on it. Withdrawing it she inspected her catch. Why, they were almost pretty, Morgana thought, but the colour was all wrong. Black snowflakes would be much better. Yes, perfect black six-pointed stars fit for a queen's crown, and Morgana smiled secretly to herself as the pure, tiny, frail whitenesses dissolved and vanished forever.

Chapter Two
Twitchwhisker and Shortpaws

In the kitchens below the Great Hall the world had gone mad. What a hustle and bustle there was! What a clattering of pots and pans as an army of cooks and kitchen staff prepared mountains of food for the coming feast.

Plump-breasted pheasants, partridges and ducks, chickens and geese by the score, roasted over blazing fires and a whole ox turned sizzling on a spit. Kitchen boys furiously stirred oceans of soup in deep cauldrons. Pastry cooks in clouds of flour kneaded and rolled acres of dough and made pies of every known kind and forests of fresh, fragrant bread. The air was thick with the tantalizing smells of richly-spiced puddings and cakes. They wafted mouth-wateringly along narrow, stone corridors and spiralled up staircases to the hall above. Here long lines of wooden tables were being prepared for the fare. Manservants and maidservants, pages and stewards scurried back and forth to make everything ready for the appointed hour. There was so much to do and the time was so short!

Sweep the floor and lay down fresh, dry straw. Hang gaily-coloured, billowing banners and deck the walls with mistletoe and holly. Polish the silver plate and burnish the goblets of gold until they gleam. Replace old candles and torches with new, that the evening be bright. So much! So much to do! Everything must be perfect! Everything must be just right for this night of deep celebration!

★　　★　　★

High above this frantic scene, on a crossbeam in the ceiling timbers, two pairs of bright eyes watched the preparations unfold.

The eyes belonged to Twitchwhisker and Shortpaws, two of the many mice which lived in Camelot. The two mice were the very best of friends and went everywhere together. Twitchwhisker was the older and larger of the two. He was a handsome young mouse with fine, silky fur, exquisitely long whiskers and a beautiful pink tail.

Compared with him, Shortpaws was a very poor specimen indeed. He had been the smallest of his litter and for a time had not been expected to live – but Shortpaws had survived and, with a little help from his great friend Twitchwhisker, he made the most of his life.

And a hard life it was for a Camelot mouse. Every day was a fight for survival. In the constant search for food, many fell victim to the dangers which lurked around every corner. Traps were laid for them by human hands, cunning snares for the foolish or unwary and, if you were wise enough to escape those, Wolfbane and his feline friends were always waiting in line.

It was of that monstrous cat that Shortpaws was thinking when he anxiously asked his friend if it wasn't time to leave. Mice never stand still for very long in one place and Shortpaws was no exception.

"Don't fuss so, Shortpaws," Twitchwhisker replied. "We've lots of time yet. Aren't you the slightest bit interested in what's happening?"

"I'm more interested in staying alive," Shortpaws replied nervously. He never felt safe when they were abroad in the vastness of Camelot. He much preferred the safety of his own hole which was small and dark and comforting.

"You worry too much," Twitchwhisker told him, unable to take his eyes off the colourful proceedings. The pomp and ceremony, which as a Camelot mouse he often witnessed, fascinated Twitchwhisker. Quite often, when he should have been busily foraging for food, he would steal time from his duties to observe them.

There was one ceremony in particular which was his firm favourite. Whenever Arthur summoned his knights to the Round Table he would find a place to watch and listen in safety as the noble king discussed his business with the gallant members. Many an hour he had lain hidden from human view listening intently as the tales of adventure were told by the tall figures seated around the fabulous table. How he longed to be one of their brave company! He saw himself riding into untold dangers at the side of Sir Galahad, Sir Gawaine or even Lancelot. He saw his personal standard flying proudly with theirs, his fiery steed prancing in step with theirs, his armour reflecting the bright sun as theirs did . . . Sir Twitchwhisker, mouse-knight of the Round Table!

"Please Twitch, let us return," Shortpaws begged.

Reluctantly, Twitchwhisker agreed. With one final

longing glimpse he followed his fearful friend along the wooden beam to the rafters and the hole which was located there.

There were many such holes in Camelot. The ancient walls were riddled with them and each one was connected to another by a network of tunnels and minute corridors that generations of mice had carefully excavated. They were the lifelines along which the ever-hungry Camelot mice scampered in search of food.

It was along a descending network which led from the roof-timbers of the Great Hall to the kitchens below that Twitchwhisker and his tiny friend scurried. Their destination was a chamber behind the vast ovens in the kitchen where they had to visit and make their report to Bede.

Bede was the oldest mouse in Camelot (at least nine years old in human time which is very old indeed for a mouse) and he was greatly respected. Wise in the ways and means of acquiring food for mouse-kind in Camelot, he held the high office of Supply Master and it was his responsibility to organize the foraging parties and supply lines which fed the mouse population. He was very wise and very grey. Some of the other young mice thought that he was a crotchety old rodent, but Twitchwhisker was devoted to him and in return the old mouse showed a great liking for the brash young mouse.

"Greetings, Bede," Twitchwhisker called out as he slid to a hurried halt with Shortpaws panting closely behind him.

"Late as usual, Twitchwhisker. When will you learn

that punctuality is a virtue any mouse can be advised to practise?'' Bede said seriously.

Twitchwhisker apologized for their late arrival and explained that they had been unavoidably detained.

''Weren't we?'' he asked Shortpaws, nudging him.

''Oh! . . . Oh, yes indeed!'' Shortpaws squeaked. ''We returned as soon as we possibly could.''

''I can imagine,'' said the old mouse. He knew when he had sent them out on their morning reconnaissance that Twitchwhisker wouldn't be able to resist lingering in order to watch the preparations for the great feast. He remembered his own mouse-youth and how he himself loved to watch the pageantry of Camelot. But that was no excuse! Duty was duty.

''What do you have to report?'' he asked sternly.

Twitchwhisker made his report. He told Bede about everything they had seen in the Great Hall. ''There should be rich pickings after the feast tonight,'' he concluded brightly, hoping that his report would pacify the old mouse.

''Quite possibly,'' replied Bede, ''but we shall not be the only ones who shall think likewise.'' Bede looked knowingly at the two young mice and they knew, without having to ask, exactly what he meant.

Wolfbane was rarely mentioned by name amongst the Camelot mice. His name struck terror into their tiny hearts. It was Wolfbane amongst all of the castle cats that the mice feared most. He was like a ghost, continually haunting the corridors, his eyes glowing like live coals. Recently the mouse casualties had been higher than usual. It was as if Wolfbane somehow knew beforehand where the foraging parties were bound. No matter how carefully their plans were laid, Wolfbane and his friends seemed always to be there, ready with fang and claw, waiting.

Now, because of the cat's success, food for the colony was in short supply and rationing had been introduced by the mouse-council. Bede looked very worried and Twitchwhisker believed the old mouse blamed himself for the desperate situation which confronted them. Starvation stared them in the face, and the prospect for winter looked very bleak. Unless their fortunes soon improved there would be many mice who would not see another Spring. Twitch-whisker desperately searched for something he could say to console Bede, but before he could, they were interrupted.

Into the chamber marched Quickstep, with Simper, his toady attendant, in tow. Quickstep was a member of the mouse-council and he was very ambitious. It was common knowledge that his sights were set firmly on Bede's office of Supply Master. A campaign of whispers against the old mouse had already begun. Twitchwhisker suspected that Simper was the source, acting under orders from Quickstep, but he couldn't prove anything. If he had had the proof he would have gladly nipped a confession out of him for Bede's sake. He felt like doing it at that moment, but his respect for Bede prevented him. Quickstep spoke up. He spoke very quickly and never wasted his words, believing that a mouse in a position of authority should get straight to the point.

"There is to be a general meeting at noon," he said. "All mice are requested to attend."

"And what is the purpose of this meeting may I ask?" Bede spoke politely.

"If you attend you shall discover that for yourself," Quickstep replied smartly. "May we count on your presence?"

"Of course," said Bede. "I have never yet neglected my duty and I do not intend to start now. Is there anything else you wish to say? I really am quite busy, Quickstep."

Quickstep looked stonily at Bede. He had been dismissed very politely by the older mouse and he did not like being dismissed by anyone.

"No, that is all," he said curtly and, fuming with anger, he turned around sharply, almost bowling over Simper in his haste to leave.

"Good riddance," Twitchwhisker said as the two mice disappeared.

"That is no way to speak about a respected member

18

of the council," Bede told him quietly. "You must learn, Twitchwhisker, to think before you speak."

"I'm sorry, Bede," Twitchwhisker apologized, "but that mouse brings out the worst in me. I don't know where you find the patience to be so polite with him."

"It comes with old age," Bede replied, "I have met other Quicksteps in my life and I daresay there will be others to follow him."

"More's the pity," Twitchwhisker said bitterly. "He is one mouse I would relish watching Wolfbane attend to personally."

"Twitch!" Shortpaws squeaked fearfully. The very mention of the dreadful name sent a shiver of fear running from his nose to the tip of his tail.

Bede looked disapprovingly at his young friend. "I think that will do," he said sharply. "Scut along to the store and draw your rations. Then try and get some sleep, you may be required for duty tonight."

Suddenly Twitchwhisker felt very ashamed of himself. He knew he had been wrong to say such a terrible thing, even if it had been in defence of Bede. He had upset Shortpaws also and was doubly miserable because of this. Sadly, he turned away to leave as he had been instructed.

"Try the bacon rind, Twitchwhisker," he heard Bede say as he went. "It's less than a week old and quite delicious."

"Thank you, Bede," Twitchwhisker replied happily. Bede was smiling once again. Twitchwhisker knew he had been forgiven for his outburst.

"Come on, Shortpaws!" he shouted, "I'll race you to the store!"

Chapter Three
Modred's Gold

As the preparations for King Arthur's feast continued at a hectic pace in Camelot, a few miles away in a secluded forest glade, a dreadful plot was being hatched.

Inside a tumbledown forester's hut, which stood beneath a giant oak tree, three men sat around a table. Two of the men were rough, rascally-looking characters. One was tall and thin with weasel-bright eyes, the other was shorter but massively built with a squat toad-like face and a large stomach which hung over his belt.

The third man was totally different from his two companions. He was as tall as the first man, with a long face and a black, pointed beard and beneath a thick winter cloak he wore the clothes of a gentleman; a tunic of rich brocade, fine silk tights and boots of soft green leather.

The wearer of the fine clothes was none other than Sir Modred and his two rascally-looking friends were notorious villains who would do anything for anyone as long as there was payment in gold at the end of the job. The thin villain was called Bandalf, the toad-faced one, Cedric. Bandalf was the cleverest of the partnership. He had all the cunning and craftiness of a fox, whereas Cedric simply obeyed orders. Cedric would cut someone's throat with less thought than a thief might cut a purse if his partner told him to. He sat silently as Bandalf discussed with Modred the task which would be undertaken that night.

"What about guards?" Bandalf was asking. "Surely Arthur will have a guard outside his chamber?"

"You will have no need to worry about the guards," Modred replied. "I have already arranged for them to be presented with a flagon of strong wine to warm them through their cold night duty."

"Drugged of course," said Bandalf. He knew all the tricks.

"Of course," Modred smiled. "Quite harmless, naturally. They will simply sleep for an hour or so. Time enough for you to slip into Arthur's chamber and dispatch him. Once done, you slip out again, closing the door behind you. The guards wake up. They've dozed off, nothing more, no need to think that anything might have happened, no need to inform the Captain of the Guard. Before Arthur's body is discovered you shall be far away. I have already personally selected two of my fastest horses for that purpose."

"How shall we get into the castle?" Bandalf enquired.

"You will deliver a hogshead of wine for the feast. My steward will be waiting with a cart for you at the crossroads. When you are admitted drive straight into the courtyard where I shall be waiting for you. You will have to hide until the feast is over. I will let you know how things are progressing and if any difficulties arise."

Bandalf nodded. "So be it. And the money?"

Modred reached into his cloak and withdrew a small leather bag. He dangled it in front of Bandalf. It looked very heavy and tantilizing. "Half now and half when it is done," Modred told Bandalf.

Bandalf took the purse and opened it. He poured out the contents. A flurry of golden coins fell down onto the rough wooden table where they sat. Bandalf gazed at the horde of shining coins in front of him and then looked up at Modred. "We shall serve you well, my lord Modred," he said.

Modred got up from the table and pulled the hood of his cloak over his head. "I'm sure you shall," he replied.

Riding back Modred congratulated himself on the arrangements he had made with Bandalf and Cedric. They had been highly recommended and the fact was, good villains were hard to find. He smiled contentedly to himself. Morgana would be very pleased. At last their plans, the hours of secret plotting, would be realized. As he rode on through the gathering snowstorm, his mind raced ahead to the future. He saw himself seated beside Morgana in the throne-room, joint ruler of the kingdom, king to her queen.

Such sweet treachery! He could hardly wait and, as if to hurry that moment along, he dug his spurs into his horse and galloped off into the enveloping whiteness in the direction of Camelot.

Chapter Four
Uproar in the Council Chamber

"Brothers! Sisters! Order please! We must have order!" Amos, the leader of the council, eventually made himself heard and the uproar in the chamber subsided into a murmur.

The commotion had been caused by Quickstep who had just finished making a speech about the drastic food situation. At the end of his speech he had said the blame could only be laid where it was due and that it lay with the Supply Master – Bede. He said that Bede was now too old for the job. A younger mouse was needed and Quickstep offered himself for that heavy duty.

The offer was a signal for the trouble to begin. Amongst those gathered in the council chamber were a group of young headstrong mice who earlier had been bribed with extra-ration promises by Simper and instructed to take up Quickstep's offer and put their voices behind him. As soon as Quickstep ceased speaking they began to chant.

"Bede is too old! Quickstep is bold! Quickstep for Supply Master!"

Influenced by the chant other mice joined in and in the uproar which followed tempers flared. There was much argument and some nipping as the supporters of Bede led by Twitchwhisker tried to silence Quickstep's cronies and it had taken quite some time to bring order to the usually orderly council meeting.

Amos waited until a respectful hush reigned over the

24

chamber before speaking again.

"Mice of Camelot, I beg you to have patience. Nothing will be solved by fighting amongst ourselves. Both sides must and will be heard. I call upon Bede to speak and answer the allegations made against him by Quickstep."

Amos stepped back and Bede slowly stepped forward to face the gathering. He looked around at the sea of faces before him. He began to speak with great dignity.

"I have listened carefully to the words of Quickstep, who we all know is an honourable mouse and much that he has said is true. I cannot deny the facts. Food is short. A hard winter we face, but to you I say we have faced hard winters before and have survived. The lot of mice is hard, that shall never change. But in order to survive we must work hard and pull together instead of fighting amongst ourselves. Nothing will be achieved if mouse is set against mouse. As to Quickstep's brave offer to relieve me of my arduous post – that is a matter for you to decide. Until you say otherwise I shall continue with my duty as I always have. Plans are ready for foraging tonight after the great feast. If fortune favours us there will be plenty for all."

Before Bede could say anything further and sensing that the old mouse might have turned the tide in his favour, Quickstep leapt forward. "Mice of Camelot, listen to me!" he squealed furiously. "Promises will not feed us! Hopes are no substitute for the food we need! I demand that a vote be taken now. Bede is too old say I. I demand a vote on this issue!"

Quickstep's demand was taken up by his supporters. They began to chant once again.

"Bede is too old! Bede is too old! Vote! Vote! We demand a vote!"

Amos managed once more, though with even greater difficulty, to call the meeting to order. He raised his paws and announced, "So it shall be. We shall vote upon the matter."

There was a burst of cheering from Quickstep's supporters and boos and hisses from Bede's.

Quickstep smiled nastily and looked triumphantly at Bede, but the old mouse remained calm and unruffled.

Amos asked those in favour of Quickstep's proposals to signify in the usual way. Paws were raised and Amos counted them. Then he asked the supporters of Bede to raise their paws. He counted once again. A buzz of excitement circulated in the chamber.

The result was very close. Finally, Amos announced that Bede had won the day — by twelve votes only. There was cheering at the announcement from Bede's supporters, especially from Twitchwhisker whose gladness was the loudest. Amos declared the meeting was ended and the crowd began to disperse. Twitchwhisker immediately went to congratulate Bede who was talking to another member of the council. He waited patiently and respectfully until they had finished, but before he could say anything to the old mouse, Bede said seriously, "Come with me."

Twitchwhisker scurried after the old mouse who showed an amazing turn of speed for his age. They left the council chamber and went to Bede's private chamber nearby. Twitchwhisker wondered why Bede was so serious? He soon found out the reason.

"Now, listen carefully you young rapscallion. There is something which I wish you to do for me. Remember that it is a request and not an order. You may refuse if you wish, for it is a mission of great danger, but one on which the survival of our colony may depend."

Twitchwhisker opened his mouth to say he would do it whatever it was, but Bede anticipated him and continued, "No, before you say anything, listen. Once you have heard what I ask of you, you may regret a

hasty decision. For many weeks now I have suspected that the success of Wolfbane and his cohorts was not simply due to their vigilance and natural cunning. There have always been cats in Camelot and they have always taken their toll of mice-kind and yet we have always managed to survive and continue. So why is it, I asked myself, that of late our casualties should be so high? Why now should our struggle be so hard? The only conclusion I can make is one which is hard to believe, but believe it I do. Wolfbane is being aided, my dear young friend. I say to you that within our midst there is a mouse who has betrayed us all!''

Twitchwhisker was stunned. A mouse in league with a cat? It was impossible to believe! Incredible! And yet he knew that Bede was not the kind of mouse to make so serious an allegation lightly.

''As yet I have no evidence, only suspicions,'' Bede admitted. ''Which brings me to my request. Later this evening I will put my plans for tonight's foraging to the council as I usually do. I want you to wait nearby and when the meeting has ended I want you to follow Quickstep.''

''Quickstep! So it's Quickstep you suspect,'' Twitchwhisker squeaked excitedly.

''Patience,'' said Bede. ''I want you to follow him and observe where he goes and who he meets. As a member of the council he will know the plans and if my suspicions prove correct soon cat-kind will know them too.''

''What do I do then?'' asked Twitchwhisker.

''You must return to me with all speed and make your report before the parties are sent on their mission. I have an alternative plan ready should it be required, after which we shall report to the council and Quickstep shall be dealt with. Well, what do you think now? Are you still eager? There will be great danger. Do you still want to do it?"

"Of course I do," Twitchwhisker replied. He had no thought at all for the dangers he might encounter. He would do anything for Bede even if it meant walking into the jaws of Wolfbane himself.

"May Shortpaws come with me?"

"I see no reason why not," Bede replied, "but you must warn him of the dangers and caution him not to squeak one word to anyone."

"Don't worry, Bede. Shortpaws can be trusted," Twitchwhisker assured him.

So it was decided and with some final advice from Bede about the dangers he might face, Twitchwhisker hurried off to find Shortpaws.

★　　★　　★

"Has the meeting finished?" Shortpaws asked sleepily, uncurling himself and stretching.

"Long ago," Twitchwhisker told him.

"Oh good," said Shortpaws, "I can go back to sleep then." He yawned a small pink yawn and snuggled down once again.

"Not so quickly, lazybones," Twitchwhisker said. He yanked Shortpaw's tail and his tiny friend squeaked with discomfort. "We've got an important mission to undertake for Bede," he added proudly.

"Mission? What kind of mission?" blinked Shortpaws.

"When you're wide awake I'll tell you," Twitchwhisker replied.

Shortpaws roused himself and listened to his friend. "I don't believe it!" he gasped when Twitchwhisker had finished. "Quickstep – a traitor. Why should he do such a thing?"

"You are slow sometimes," Twitchwhisker said shaking his head. "Who stands to win if Wolfbane continues to be so successful? Who wants Bede's job? Quickstep, that's who, and he's the kind of mouse who wouldn't let anything stand in his way."

"But helping Wolfbane, that's terrible, Twitch! It's unthinkable. Perhaps Bede is mistaken?"

"Perhaps. But how often have you known Bede to be wrong?" said Twitchwhisker. "I'll wager my life that he's right."

"You might be doing just that," Shortpaws said fearfully.

"So you're not coming along?"

"I didn't say that," Shortpaws hurriedly replied.

"Well, are you?"

"I suppose so," answered Shortpaws.

"Try not to sound so pleased about it," Twitchwhisker teased. "Just think what this will do for your reputation. Why, you could become a hero overnight."

"I could become something else overnight also."

"And what might that be?" asked Twitch.

"Don't ask," replied Shortpaws. "Please *just* don't ask, you might end up having to drag me out of here."

But Twitchwhisker knew who his small friend was

thinking about. Wolfbane was never far from Shortpaws' thoughts.

Following Bede's instructions, Twitchwhisker and Shortpaws waited and then, as the appointed time for the meeting approached, they made their way to Amos' private chamber where it was due to be held. Nearby they found a convenient hole and settled down to watch and wait, hidden from view but perfectly able to see the entrance to the chamber.

They quietly observed the council members arriving. Bede was deep in conversation with two other members as he arrived. Then Quickstep approached with Simper close behind. Twitchwhisker strained his ears to catch the whispered words which passed between the two mice. They were too far away. Whatever Quickstep said to Simper remained a secret. Whatever it was though sent Simper hurrying off and Quickstep disappeared into the chamber.

By the time the meeting was concluded and the members began to emerge Shortpaws was fast asleep and Twitchwhisker was stiff with waiting. "Wake up," he whispered to his sleeping friend.

Together they watched as council members left to return to their own chambers.

"There's Quickstep!" Twitchwhisker exclaimed quietly. "Quickly, Shortpaws, we mustn't lose him."

Down dark corridors at a safe distance they followed him. Quickstep was living up to his name as he hurried along at a terrific pace through the gloom. Soon they were beyond the colony area and scurrying along a series of passages which gradually led upwards to the level above the kitchens.

"Come on, Shortpaws," Twitchwhisker squeaked urgently. "We must keep up with him."

"My paws are dropping off," moaned Shortpaws.

Twitchwhisker paid no attention to his friend's complaint. He was too busy concentrating on the small dark figure of Quickstep hurrying ahead. On and on they went through a maze of tunnels, the followed and the followers.

"He's heading for the Armoury," Twitchwhisker informed Shortpaws.

"The Armoury?" puffed Shortpaws. "Why should he want to go there?"

"Can you think of a better place for a secret meeting?" Twitchwhisker asked. "It's just as Bede said – Quickstep is up to mischief. Hurry now, he's almost there!"

Chapter Five
The Meeting in the Armoury

Tornear, Wolfbane's lieutenant, pricked up his one good ear at the sound of approaching paws. "Our tiny friend has arrived," he purred.

Wolfbane's eyes opened to mere slits and he smiled as only a cat can smile. "As punctual as usual," he observed sleepily. "Let us hope that he has something interesting to tell us — for *his* sake!"

Tornear mewed fiendishly as the mouse-shape of Quickstep scampered towards them, dwarfed on all sides by the standing suits of polished armour which stood like silent giants along the length of the Armoury.

"Greetings, Wolfbane," Quickstep said when he reached them.

Wolfbane nodded a silent acknowledgement. He looked at his lieutenant.

"Well, Quickstep, be brief," said Tornear. "What news do you bring?"

"I have the plans for the foraging after tonight's feast," Quickstep replied breathlessly.

"Very interesting," Tornear said. "You have done well."

"Thank you," replied the mouse. "I wish only to serve you."

Wolfbane chuckled deeply, breaking his silence. "Do you think we are fools, mouseling? You serve only yourself. You use us for your own ends."

34

"I assure you, Wolfbane . . ." Quickstep began to splutter.

"Assure us of nothing!" Wolfbane hissed menacingly, unsheathing a pawful of claws. "Simply tell us the plans and then you may go."

Quickstep gulped. Only his ambition for power kept him from taking to his paws.

"Well?" asked Tornear.

Quickstep wasted no more time. "Bede plans a two-pronged attack. Shortly after the feast is over and human-kind are abed, two groups of mice will set out to forage. The first party is to act as a decoy. Bede plans that they will draw you away from the hall and whilst you are occupied with the chase the second party will carry off the remains of the feast."

"Bede shows great cunning," Wolfbane said, "I am very impressed. Is there anything else we should know?"

Quickstep shook his head.

"Then you may go," Wolfbane smiled.

Quickstep turned and began to hurry away, but before he got very far Wolfbane flicked out a paw and trapped the mouse's tail to the stone floor.

"I hope for your sake, Quickstep, that what you have told us is the truth. I would hate to discover that you are lying. I'm afraid I would be very angry, very angry indeed, and I don't think you would like me when I am angry."

"It's the truth, I swear it!" Quickstep squeaked fearfully. He could feel Wolfbane's hot breath and his tail pained him badly.

Suddenly Wolfbane stiffened. Quickstep and

Tornear heard it also – a scuffling at the far end of the Armoury.

"Tornear!" said Wolfbane. Wolfbane's lieutenant needed no further instruction. As silently as a shadow he padded away, slinking low as cats do when they are hunting.

"Stay here," hissed Wolfbane to Quickstep. He followed Tornear on a parallel course. Halfway down he stopped and sniffed the air. Mouse! He could smell mouse! He could smell the fear of mouse-kind. That most delicious scent! Where were they? And how many? Wolfbane stalked forward cautiously ready to pounce when Tornear flushed them out.

All at once there they were! Tornear leapt and two mice broke cover, scampering swiftly away from their pursuer towards the door of the Armoury. Wolfbane saw immediately the gap between the floor and the door. It was the tiniest gap, but nevertheless large enough for escape. Wolfbane hurled himself at the door hoping to cut them off. He was too late! The mice were swifter than he had imagined and as he reached the door their tails flicked out of sight and they were gone.

Withdrawing his claws from the wood of the door, Wolfbane swirled around to face the trembling Quickstep. His eyes were blazing with anger.

"You have been careless, Quickstep," he said, retracing his steps. "It appears you were followed. What do you have to say for yourself?"

Tornear joined him and together they towered over their shivering informant.

"You must go after them as quickly as possible," gibbered Quickstep. "I know those two mice. They are in the pay of Bede. If they escape, Bede will call off his plans for tonight."

"Must!" snarled Wolfbane. "Do you dare to tell us what we must do, Quickstep?"

"Of course not," the terrified mouse replied. "I assure you . . ."

"Assuring us again, mouseling. I grow tired of your assurances and when I am tired I grow bad-tempered. Do I not, Tornear?"

"Indeed," replied Wolfbane's lieutenant.

Quickstep looked from one set of eyes to the other, eyes which blazed above him like twin sets of fiendish lamps. He glanced towards the gap under the Armoury door. One quick dash and he would be free!

It was a vain attempt. He was hardly past Wolfbane when a powerfully vicious paw scooped him high into the air. He turned once, twice, like an acrobat and then landed heavily on the cold stone floor.

"Poor Quickstep," purred Wolfbane. "Such a pity that it had to end this way."

"What now?" Tornear enquired.

"Why, after our two runaways of course," Wolfbane replied. "We wouldn't want a change in plans now would we? We owe that to Quickstep, do we not?"

"Most assuredly," Tornear replied, and without another word the two cats leapt for the open window of the Armoury and disappeared into the gathering darkness outside, leaving behind the tiny lifeless shape of Quickstep and his guard of metal giants.

★　　★　　★

When he was certain that they were quite safe, and not being followed, Twitchwhisker slowed down.

Shortpaws collapsed in a heap at his side. "That was the most terrible experience of my life," he gasped.

"I warned you that it could be dangerous," said Twitchwhisker. He laughed for his small friend's benefit and for his own. They had escaped death by a whisker and yet he felt strangely glad and excited by it all. It was the very stuff of adventure and he loved it.

"What are we going to do now?" Shortpaws enquired.

"We must report back to Bede as soon as possible. The foragers must not set off. The only trouble is I'm slightly lost."

"Lost!" Shortpaws echoed despairingly. "Oh, Twitch, don't say that!"

"Calm yourself," Twitchwhisker replied confidently. "We'll get back home one way or another.

Count on me."

Having rested and recovered their senses the two small adventurers set off once again. They found themselves in a long, well-lit corridor hung with rich tapestries. Cautiously they made their way towards the end of the corridor, constantly alert for human or cat-kind.

"Twitch, someone's coming!" squeaked Shortpaws.

They scampered towards a nearby door and took cover. Past them swept a pair of human legs on seemingly urgent business. (Actually it was a squire to one of King Arthur's knights hurrying to his master who was preparing himself for the great feast which was due to start soon.)

"He's gone, Twitch, we're safe," Shortpaws breathed easily. "Shall we go?"

"Wait. Not yet." Twitchwhisker had his ear to the door.

"What is it?" Shortpaws asked. He was eager to be away and return to his safe hole back in the colony.

"Ssh!" Twitchwhisker commanded, almost angrily. He listened for a few moments more. "Someone's talking about the king."

"So what?" Shortpaws squeaked anxiously. He cared nothing for the concerns of human-kind, king or kitchen boy they were all the same – something to be avoided at all costs.

"I want to investigate. I don't like the sound of this."

"Please, Twitch, no. We have to return and report to Bede. You said so yourself."

"It won't take a moment. Come on."

There was nothing Shortpaws could do. He knew that when Twitchwhisker made up his mind about doing something all the argument in the world wouldn't budge him from his intentions. He reluctantly followed his friend who was already halfway under the door.

They emerged into a darkly-lit chamber full of deep shadows and quickly took cover behind a large wooden chest which stood near the door.

The voices were much louder now. They belonged to a man and a woman who were seated at a table in the centre of the room. Twitchwhisker worked his way silently towards the end of the chest and peered around it. Shortpaws stayed exactly where he was. He wanted to stay close to the door.

"Who is it, Twitch?" he whispered to his curious friend.

Twitch did not reply. He was listening to the conversation which passed between the human-kind and what he heard made his heart beat wildly and his whiskers dance.

Strange are the tricks played by Fate. Sent on a mission to uncover the treachery of a brother mouse, they had accidently uncovered even greater treachery. For what the two humans were discussing so casually was nothing less than the killing of a king; they were discussing the death of King Arthur himself!

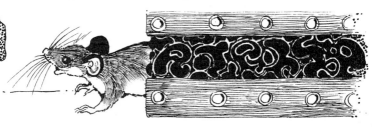

Chapter Six
The Deadly Conversation

Unaware that their treachery was being observed Morgana lifted her goblet of wine and proposed a toast to Sir Modred. "Let us drink to success," she smiled. "Let us drink to my dear step-brother Arthur."

Sir Modred lifted his goblet and clinked it ceremoniously against Morgana's. "Long may he reign," he replied sarcastically.

Morgana laughed and drank deeply. Somehow the wine tasted especially sweet on this occasion. The news Modred had brought to her was good indeed and if things went according to plan soon she would be proclaimed queen. No one would oppose her. Arthur did not have an heir and she was his closest relative. It was the law – the kingdom would go to her. After a suitable period of mourning for her dear, dead, step-brother, Modred would make the arrangements for her coronation and the crown would be hers.

Then she would show them! She would show them all how a kingdom should be ruled. First of all she would deal with Guinevere, Arthur's wife. Poor Guinevere! So young to be a widow. Of course she would have to leave Camelot. Perhaps I will send her to a nunnery, Morgana mused. It would be the proper thing to do. After all she would need peace and solitude to recover from her grief, a quiet place to reflect on her life.

After Guinevere she would turn her attention to

Arthur's close friends, his most faithful knights and that old fool Merlin. It would be easy to dispose of them. Merlin might have a nasty fall on the spiral staircase which led up to his chamber or perhaps he might eat something which did not agree with him. As for the knights – for those who found it hard to serve Morgana as she required them to do there would be long quests and impossible missions which would keep them away for years and when they returned eventually (if they did at all, for who knows the dangers that might await them?) they would find that Camelot had changed. She would make new knights, loyal to her alone, to take their places. Modred would choose them. She knew she could rely upon him to find the very best for her purposes.

She would rule her kingdom with fire and sword, replacing love of a king with fear of a queen. Yes. Fear was the key. Forget about justice and honour and gallantry and chivalry and the rights of the people to lead happy, peaceful lives! Put fear into their hearts. Make them aware that the slightest opposition to her word would be swiftly and brutally dealt with; tax them to the limit and then tax them even more. Break their spirits and grind them down until they became slaves to her will!

And with the kingdom hers she would turn her attentions to her neighbours. Other kingdoms, long at peace under Arthur's reign, were waiting to be plucked like ripe fruit. From Arthur's once peaceful kingdom she would reach out and her power would spread throughout the land until she possessed it all. She saw it all so clearly – the vast empire stretching as far as the eye could see and it would all begin that night after the feast was finished.

Little wonder that the wine tasted so rich and full of sweetness.

"Tell me again, Modred," said Morgana. "I want to know every detail. I want to savour them as we sit at Arthur's table. I want to feed off the promise of things to come."

Modred repeated the plans he had made with Bandalf and Cedric.

"Are you certain these men can be trusted?"

"Do not worry my queen-to-be," Modred replied. "They shall play their parts to perfection. Naturally, once the deed is done there will have to be a slight change in plan. It would be unwise, I'm sure you would agree, to allow them to live. Tongues wag eventually and secrets are made known. I'm afraid that as they ride out, with Arthur's blood on their hands, they will be challenged by a force of my men and in their attempt to escape justice they will be cut down by hand-picked archers."

"You have thought of everything, my lord," said Morgana happily. She drank the last of her wine and putting down her goblet took up a magnificent black cloak of rich fur from her bed. Modred held it out for her and she slipped it over her shoulders. She danced away and held herself for Modred's inspection.

"How do I look, Sir Modred?"

"Fit to be a queen, my lady," he replied with dreadful gallantry.

Morgana laughed harshly. "Then what must be, must be. Let us go, Sir Knight. The feast and the king

await us.'' She took Sir Modred's arm and they left the chamber, Morgana blowing out the black candles as she went, plunging it into darkness.

At the end of the corridor Morgana espied her pet, Wolfbane. She bent down and picked him up. "And where have you been, my naughty precious?" she asked rubbing her nose to his. "Come, I have left a bowl of fresh cream for you."

Morgana carried the cat back to her chamber and opening the door she pushed him inside, before returning to her escort and proceeding to the feast.

Hardly daring to breathe, Twitchwhisker and Shortpaws stood as still as statues beneath the canopy of Morgana's bed. They knew that the slightest false move would alert Wolfbane to their presence. They had run under the bed in panic when Morgana had returned so unexpectedly with her dreadful cargo, who was now busily engaged with the bowl of cream which his mistress had left for him.

"Twitch, what are we to do?" Shortpaws whispered, trying to stop his teeth from chattering.

"Ssh! Let me think. Don't talk so much. Wolfbane might hear us."

The mention of Wolfbane immediately silenced the petrified mouse. He turned to stone once again and waited for Twitchwhisker to think of some way out of their perilous predicament.

Feverishly, Twitchwhisker considered their situation. They had fallen out of the frying pan into the fire. So much depended upon their return to the colony. Bede was counting upon them and now there was the question of the plot against the king. He had no idea what he could do about that yet, but he was determined to do something.

But the first thing they had to do was to get out of Morgana's chamber, away from Wolfbane. Retracing their steps to the door was out of the question. That route would take them too close to Wolfbane. He had only to turn and he would have them.

The only alternative was the chamber window. If they could make it to the window without discovery they would have a chance at least, though once there who knew what awaited them? Beyond the window was the Great Outside which was how the mice of Camelot referred to the world outside the comforting stones of the castle. Camelot mice rarely ventured into the open air. The Great Outside was an alien world to them, full of frightful dangers according to mouse-legend.

Nevertheless that was the route which Twitchwhisker chose. Time was ticking away and they had to get back before the foraging parties were sent out. He nudged Shortpaws and beckoned silently to him. The two mice crept silently beneath the dark cave of the bed to the opposite side and closer to the window.

Half covering the window was a dark curtain made of thick woollen material. Twitchwhisker whispered instructions to Shortpaws and at his signal they ran towards the curtain and flung themselves at it, digging their tiny claws into the material, and began the climb upwards towards the window ledge.

It was hard going even though mice are good climbers. The curtain swayed from side to side as they ascended slowly on its outer edge. It hissed against the stone as it swayed and seemed to make a terrible noise. Once they stopped when they heard Wolfbane yawn and stretch himself. If he had turned at that moment all would have been lost, but he was too interested in the cream Morgana had left for him. The mice continued their climb.

At last they reached the window ledge and Twitchwhisker pulled Shortpaws up after him. They quickly took cover behind the curtain. The night wind ruffled their fur and a few flakes of snow, blown inward, fell on them. It was very cold. The storm had almost blown itself out now. A thick layer of snow lay everywhere. The towers and battlements of Camelot looked like some kind of fantastic iced cake and the courtyard below was a deep white meadow.

"Twitch, I'm scared," Shortpaws squeaked. They were very high up and the night seemed so dark and vast and he felt so small that what courage he possessed had completely deserted him.

"Don't worry," Twitchwhisker whispered to him. "We're going to be all right. Look, we can go this way."

Leading away from the window ledge was another narrower ledge which travelled along the outside of the tower wherein Morgana's chamber stood.

"Follow me and stay close," he told Shortpaws. "I shall go first. Be careful not to slip." He had hardly given the warning when he heard Shortpaws cry out loudly and turned to see his small friend clinging to the edge of the ledge by his paw tips.

"Help! Twitch, help! I can't hold on!"

Twitchwhisker leapt into action. He grabbed for Shortpaws and clutched hold of a pawful of fur behind his neck. "Pull yourself up!" Twitchwhisker squeaked, hauling in his companion with all his strength. "Pull! Pull!"

With a supreme effort, Shortpaws was returned to the safety of the ledge. It was then, at that moment of rescue, that Twitchwhisker saw the big yellow eye.

Wolfbane was on the window ledge! The frightened cries of Shortpaws had attracted him. Twitchwhisker grabbed his friend's paw and they scuttled out of reach. As they reached the corner of the tower he turned and saw that the cat was on their trail, edging carefully along the ledge after them.

Turning the corner in a flurry of snow they ran on. The ledge led to the battlements. As they reached the end Wolfbane turned the corner!

"There's nothing else for it, Shortpaws. We'll have to jump," said Twitchwhisker. The battlements stood beneath them. A human could have reached out and touched them, but for a mouse it was a leap of tremendous proportions.

"I can't do it!" squeaked Shortpaws, holding himself back.

"You have to!" Twitchwhisker shouted. Wolfbane was almost upon them. Twitchwhisker took his friend's trembling paw and without another word launched himself for the battlements!

49

The layer of snow on the stone cushioned their fall, but they could not control their landing. They slid over the stone and careered towards the edge of the battlements. Suddenly there was nothing beneath their paws and they were falling, tumbling head over tail through the darkness. The wind whistled in their ears and the walls of Camelot flashed past them in a blur. Down and down they fell for what seemed like an eternity.

"Twitch!" Shortpaws' fearful cry rang in the night.

Then they hit the cold waters of the moat. A tiny column of water shot upwards and they disappeared beneath the surface. For a few moments nothing could be seen, then two small heads surfaced, gasping for air.

"Swim for the bank!" Twitchwhisker commanded.

"I shan't make it," Shortpaws squealed.

"Then drown!" Twitchwhisker snapped, finally losing his temper with his friend.

The prospect of a watery death shocked Shortpaws into action and he struck out for the bank opposite the castle walls, following in the wake of Twitchwhisker.

Exhausted and cold they dragged themselves wearily onto the bank and flopped into the snow.

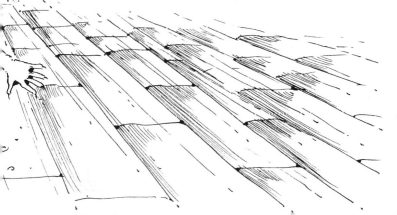

Twitchwhisker looked back towards the battlements which loomed above them across the waters of the moat. Silhouetted on them he could see Wolfbane, his tail swishing angrily and his eyes blazing. A high-pitched yowl curled into the night and then Wolfbane was gone.

Twitchwhisker breathed a sigh of relief. They were safe once again. Twice they had escaped Wolfbane. Few mice could say that. He wondered whether their paths would cross again? Hopefully not. At his side Shortpaws stirred. He looked very miserable.

"I told you we would make it, didn't I?" Twitchwhisker said brightly. "Don't look so glum. All we've got to do now is get back into the castle."

Shortpaws hung his head. "I'm sorry for all the trouble I've caused you, Twitch," he apologized. "You would have been better off without me."

"Nonsense!" Twitchwhisker quickly replied. "It takes two to go adventuring. I'm glad I asked you to come along. Dangers are made for sharing aren't they? Come on, let's find the drawbridge. It's the only way back into the castle. There's no more time to waste. Onward mice!"

Feeling much better Shortpaws echoed Twitchwhisker's words. He was determined to be brave despite the dangers which lay ahead. "Onward!" he squeaked and off they set through the deep snow.

It was whilst Bede was waiting patiently for Twitchwhisker to return and make his report that Simper suddenly burst into his chamber. There was a wild look in his eyes, an expression of terror, and he was panting heavily. "Bede, help me! *Please* help me!" he squeaked piteously.

Before Bede could make any reply and ask the frightened mouse what he wanted four more young mice burst in and dashed up to Simper. They began to set about him, nipping and scratching him badly. Simper squealed and begged for mercy.

"Stop this instantly!" thundered Bede. He leapt in between Simper and his attackers.

"Out of the way, Bede," the leader of the gang, a powerfully-built mouse with a scarred lip, said menacingly to the old mouse. "This has nothing to do with you. Give Simper to us and we shall leave you in peace."

Bede stood his ground. He faced the intruders with a determined expression. "And I tell you, that you will stop this disgraceful behaviour immediately or I shall call for assistance and you will face stiff punishment for trespassing and assault on a brother mouse."

Bede's words of warning calmed the gang down. They backed away. Bede was now in full command. "Now," he said, "tell me what this is all about."

"Ask him!" replied the leader. He pointed an accusing paw at Simper who was cowering in a corner, snivelling to himself.

Bede turned around to face the unfortunate mouse. "Perhaps you had better tell me," he said to Simper.

"You must believe me, Bede, he made me do it! He *made* me!" Simper whined.

"Who made you do what?"

"Quickstep," Simper continued. "He made me help him."

"Go on," said Bede.

Simper told the whole story. It came tumbling out. A cascading confession of words. He told how, almost six months previously, Quickstep had caught him in the act of stealing supplies from the stores, but instead of reporting the theft to the council (an offence which could have resulted in expulsion from Camelot into the Great Outside) Quickstep had blackmailed Simper into helping him disgrace Bede. Quickstep had forced him to act as go-between, taking messages to and from cat-kind, arranging meetings and so forth. It was Quickstep who had instructed him to start the campaign of scurrilous whispers against Bede and to bribe the mice to make trouble at the general meeting held earlier that day.

"Is this true?" Bede asked the young mice.

"We were promised extra rations," the leader replied. "It was only a bit of fun. But now he's gone back on his word — that's why we came after him." He glared at Simper.

"I can't get them!" Simper squeaked. "I can't get them until Quickstep returns!"

"And where is your master now?" Bede asked.

"I don't know," Simper wailed. "I haven't seen him since this evening. He should have returned from a meeting with Wolfbane by now."

"And where was this meeting to be held?"

"In the Armoury. Quickstep instructed me to arrange a meeting at the Armoury."

"I see," Bede said thoughtfully. He turned to the other mice. "Listen to me," he said to them. "I want you first to go to Amos and the other members of the council and ask them to come here as soon as they can. When you have done that I want you to go and find Quickstep and bring him here also. You may use any means you wish to do so, for doubtless he will object. I should start at the Armoury first."

The gang put their heads together and whispered amongst themselves. Finally the leader addressed Bede. "If we do this, what will happen to us?" he asked.

"I promise you that your small and foolish part in this disgraceful episode will be looked upon mercifully by the council. You have the word of Bede that no action will be taken against you."

The mice agreed and went off to do Bede's bidding. Shortly afterwards, Amos and the other members of the council appeared. When all had arrived Bede told Simper to tell them the whole story once again. Amos and the others were shocked by what they heard. Never before in the history of Camelot mice-kind had such treachery been known.

"We must, of course, cancel the plans for tonight's foraging," Amos told Bede.

"I have already prepared alternative plans," Bede replied. He told Amos how he had suspected Quickstep for some time and how he had sent Twitchwhisker and Shortpaws to gather proof of treachery and confessed that he was very worried about their safety.

"I shouldn't worry too much," Amos said. "Twitchwhisker is a clever young rascal."

As they spoke, word arrived that Quickstep had been found.

"Bring him in," Amos ordered.

Quickstep was brought in. He was laid before them.

"Such is the price of treachery," Bede observed sadly.

Amos ordered the body to be taken away and buried without honour or ceremony. After further discussion Bede was left alone. He reflected on the recent events. So his suspicions had proved to be correct. Quickstep was no more. His ambition and lust for power had brought about his downfall.

But what about Twitchwhisker and Shortpaws? What had happened to them? Dread filled Bede's old heart. Twitchwhisker had gone so brightly and willingly on the mission for him and perhaps somewhere even now they lay, cold and still, victims of Wolfbane or some other cruel claws. If that was so, he would never be able to forgive himself . . .

With these sad thoughts, Bede left his chamber to issue new instructions for the foraging. As he wearily made his way along dark corridors, sounds of merriment, of music and songs and gay laughter filtered down from the Great Hall high above. The feast to celebrate Christmas had begun, but Bede did not hear them, his thoughts were elsewhere, he was with two small mice, two small brave mice . . . somewhere.

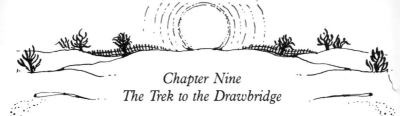

As Bede went on his sad way about his duties the two creatures who occupied his thoughts so completely were ploughing their way through white wheatfields of snow towards the drawbridge.

Their plunge into the moat had left them at the rear of the castle, at a point furthest away from the only entrance and with the daunting prospect of a trek halfway around the familiar walls in order to reach safety.

The going was very hard. The snow was very deep in places and the wind was bitterly cold. Under the pale eye of a December moon the two mice made their way. Twitchwhisker led and Shortpaws followed in the furrow of his passage. As they went along, Twitchwhisker tried to keep up their spirits by talking non-stop. He talked about anything and everything, hoping that it would somehow shorten their journey and make Shortpaws forget the dangers which possibly lay ahead.

"Just wait until we get back," he piped up cheerily. "Think of the stories we'll be able to tell. I shouldn't be at all surprised if we become part of mouse-legend overnight. They'll tell tales about us for years to come. How we survived two meetings with Wolfbane and managed to keep our tails when all around were losing theirs. Think about it, Shortpaws, we'll be heroes."

Shortpaws didn't feel like a hero. He felt cold and miserable and very tired. He felt himself to be exactly

58

what he was — a small, frightened mouse on the Great Outside, though he tried not to show it to Twitchwhisker. "How much further?" he asked as brightly as he possibly could.

"We're almost there," Twitchwhisker replied. That was only a guess. He didn't know exactly how far they had gone or how much time had passed since their escape from Wolfbane. They had to press on regardless of the cold and the danger.

He wondered, as he trod on, what Quickstep would do when he returned? Treason towards mouse-kind would be rewarded with exile from Camelot. Without a doubt, Quickstep had seen them in the Armoury. Perhaps he would try to stop them reporting to Bede? Who could say what would happen? Twitchwhisker decided that he would worry about that when they got into the castle.

Through the dark night the two friends travelled. The journey grew harder with each step. Their paws were freezing. On and on they went through the crisp white snow. Above their heads, thousands of stars glinted like silver coins in a vast black purse. It was a strange new world this Great Outside, a world of white yet a world of shadows and dark shapes from whence threatened to pounce the unimaginable horrors of mouse-legends.

Nevertheless onwards they pressed, tunnelling their way through deep drifts, two small creatures cast by circumstance on the Great Outside. As they passed by a small copse of trees, high above them there was a soundless ruffling of feathers. The moon-round large eyes blinked open. A tawny owl lifted its head and looked down. With growing interest it watched as the two mice passed beneath. Recognizing a meal the owl opened its wings and silently flitted from its roost to another tree beneath which the two weary travellers would have to pass.

"What was that?" Shortpaws squeaked. He had heard the softest whooshing of wind.

"It's just the wind," Twitchwhisker said. "Come on, it's not much further now."

As they approached its perch the owl prepared itself. One swift, soundless dive and it would feast royally. It launched itself into the cold night air. Once it circled and then the great rounded wings folded inward and it fell towards its victims.

Shortpaws did not ask this time what the sound was. He looked around and up into the night sky. Against the glittering background of stars he saw the winged terror swooping down. A fearful cry leapt into his throat. "Twitch look out! Look out!"

Now Twitchwhisker turned and saw too. He saw the cruel talons opened ready to clutch. He saw the cruel beak gaping wide. He saw the yellow eyes blazing with death and for a split-second he was rooted to the spot — but only for a split-second. As the claws swept towards them and the wings braked the dive, he pushed Shortpaws to one side with all his strength and leapt in the opposite direction himself.

His quick thinking saved both their lives. As he landed in a small drift he heard the sound of a heavy object landing in the snow. Beating wings raised a storm of snowflakes. Clumsily the owl floundered around trying to free itself for flight.

Twitchwhisker wasted no time. "This way!" he shouted to Shortpaws, and scuttled as fast as his paws could carry him towards the nearest tree. Shortpaws was not far behind. Luck was with them once more and they found a gap in the trunk which was large enough for them to squeeze through. They were safe for the time being at least. "It was a good thing you saw it," Twitchwhisker said. "Another moment and it would have had us for sure."

"Did you see those eyes?" Shortpaws rolled his own fearfully. "I've never seen eyes like those before and I certainly never want to again. What is it doing now?"

Twitchwhisker cautiously crept to the entrance and peeked outside. He was just in time to see the owl finally managing to lift off from the snow. Like a ghost it spirited itself away with a few broad strokes of its wings and disappeared into the darkness.

"All clear," Twitchwhisker informed him, "but we'd better wait in case it decides to come back for a second try."

Shortpaws readily agreed and they waited inside the tree trunk. After what seemed an age, Twitchwhisker cautiously stepped outside and took a look around. The owl was nowhere to be seen. Twitchwhisker called Shortpaws to follow him.

"Are you sure it's safe?"

"It's as safe as it will ever be," replied Twitchwhisker. Although the owl was nowhere to be seen, that did not necessarily mean that it could not see them; that it was not waiting to swoop once again. It would be a chance they had to take. Eventually, Shortpaws emerged from the safety of the tree and they set off for the drawbridge once again. Before long they reached their goal and took shelter thankful that their trek was now over. The next thing to do was to get into the castle. At the far end of the drawbridge, sheltering beneath the arched entrance to the courtyard, stood two sentries.

"What do we do now?" whispered Shortpaws.

"We'll have to wait and hope that we can sneak past them. They might fall asleep or go inside. Just be patient. We've come this far. Nothing can stop us now."

They waited once again. The sentries showed no signs of moving or of falling asleep at their post. Twitchwhisker began to grow impatient. Should they make a dash and try their luck? Perhaps they wouldn't be seen . . . Before he had to make a decision, fate stepped in to save them. They heard a rumbling sound in the distance. Coming slowly towards them, drawn by a seedy-looking nag, came a cart. On the driving seat sat two men and behind them, cradled carefully, was a large barrel — a hogshead of wine.

As the cart approached the sentries left their posts and came to the end of the drawbridge. One of them held up his hand and the cart pulled to a halt. "State your business," he said.

"Wine for good King Arthur's feast," the driver of the cart replied.

The second guard inspected the cargo. He knocked the barrel with his dagger hilt. It sounded full.

"We were not told to expect you," said the first guard. He eyed the driver suspiciously. "No one passes unless they are expected."

"Perhaps not," the driver replied, "but I was ordered to deliver it. If you won't let me pass then you shall explain to your masters why there was no wine for the feast." He began to back up the cart in order to turn around.

"Let them in," said the second guard. He didn't want any trouble. "It's only wine they bring."

Grudgingly the first guard agreed. He stood to one side. The driver cracked his whip and the nag started forward over the drawbridge.

Unknown to all four men the cart now carried two tiny stowaways. Whilst the cart had been at a standstill, Twitchwhisker, seeing an opportunity not to be missed, acted quickly. Suspended from the back of the cart was a length of rope which almost touched the ground. It was an easy matter for the two mice to scuttle silently across and climb up it into the cart.

Thus the last obstacle was crossed and the mice rode safely into Camelot. Neither of the mice knew though that the humans who provided their transport were Bandalf and Cedric who had just completed the first part of Modred's dastardly plan. It was not until the cart passed into the courtyard and a shadowy figure called out softly to them from a darkened doorway that Twitchwhisker realized who they must be.

Bandalf reined in the nag and jumped down from the driving seat, quickly followed by Cedric.

"This way," whispered the dark figure. A door opened and light fell upon the cruel features of Modred. So these must be the two who will carry out the dirty deed, Twitchwhisker thought. His tiny heart swelled with anger. Oh to be bigger and have a sword

in hand! He would leap amongst them and cut them down like the treacherous, black-hearted dogs they were.

The terrible trio went inside and a few moments later Modred reappeared and returned to the feast. Certain that the coast was clear, Twitchwhisker led Shortpaws in the climb down the rope. They dropped silently into the thick carpet of snow.

"Hurry, Shortpaws," called Twitchwhisker as he scuttled off in the direction of the kitchens. "There's not a moment to lose!"

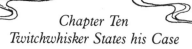

A hero's reception awaited the two adventurers. As soon as they reached the colony boundaries, which they did without further incident, they were greeted by Ezekiel, a council steward, and were hurried off to the council chamber where the mice of Camelot had gathered to hear Bede's telling of recent events.

Amidst great cheering the two friends were ushered before the assembly and Twitchwhisker was asked to relate their side of the story. When he had completed his tale (having left out the plot of Modred and Morgana which he wished only to discuss with Bede when the opportunity arose) Amos stepped forward and addressed the mice with a speech praising to high heaven the courage and daring, the enterprise and devotion to duty shown by Twitchwhisker and Shortpaws and promised that their endeavours would be well rewarded when the desperate situation Camelot mice faced was finally resolved.

Once again the chamber rang with the cheers and hurrahs of the mice, cheers which would have continued indefinitely if Amos had not called the meeting to an end and asked the mice to return to their duties.

Twitchwhisker and Shortpaws went off with Bede to his chamber where he provided them with food and they talked further of their adventures.

"I began to believe that I would never see you again," Bede confessed. "When Quickstep's body was brought back I feared that Wolfbane had taken you also."

"He almost did," Twitchwhisker said.

"Twice!" squeaked Shortpaws, with a note of triumph.

Bede smiled happily. "Well now, you must be greatly tired. I suggest that you return to your holes and sleep. We can talk again at a later time."

"There was something else which I wanted to talk to you about," Twitchwhisker said quickly.

"And what might that be?" asked Bede.

Twitchwhisker told him about the plot he and Shortpaws had overheard in Morgana's room.

Bede looked very serious. He guessed what Twitchwhisker was thinking even before the young mouse spoke of it. "And you wish to do something to help the king, do you not?"

"Naturally," said Twitchwhisker. "The king is good and just, you have said so yourself. Modred must be stopped at all costs."

"And how do you intend to stop him?" Bede asked. "What can mouse kind do against human-kind? No, my young friend, it would be foolhardy to try. You have already risked your life enough for one day. Forget the king, Twitchwhisker. His fate is not your concern."

"But they're going to kill him, Bede! Surely we shouldn't let that happen." Twitchwhisker found it hard to believe what he was hearing. Bede was saying that they should do nothing, that they should stand by and allow Arthur, the noblest of all human-kind he knew, to be murdered in his bed!

"Mouse-kind have never involved themselves in the affairs of human-kind," retorted Bede. "You would be throwing away your life in order to try and save a human life. Do you think that a human would do the same for a mouse?"

"I don't care about that!" exclaimed Twitchwhisker. "Please, Bede, I have to try!"

Old Bede sighed deeply. He knew he would not be able to convince his young friend of the folly of his intentions. "I could forbid you to go," he said. "What would you do then?"

"Then I would have to disobey you for the first time in my life," Twitchwhisker promptly answered.

Bede shook his head. "You are a headstrong, foolish young mouse," he said. He crossed his chamber and, reaching into a hole in the wall, withdrew from it a scroll of paper which looked very ancient and dusty. He carried it back to Twitchwhisker and blowing the dust off, gently unrolled it.

"Since you are determined to undertake this mad adventure I suggest you pay close attention to what you see here before you."

"What is it?" Twitchwhisker asked. He drew closer to the old mouse and peered over his shoulder.

"It is a plan, mouseling. A plan of Camelot. Made many generations ago by one of my ancestors. He copied it from the original human-kind plans used during the building of the castle. Now here is the North Tower wherein lies the king's chamber. The safest way for you to go is thus." And Bede traced out a route with his paw, a route which skirted around the Great Hall.

"But that isn't the shortest way," protested Twitchwhisker. "Surely if I cross the hall it will halve my journey?"

Bede nodded in agreement. "Most certainly it will, but you must sacrifice distance for safety's sake. The hall and the surrounding area will be patrolled tonight by Wolfbane and his friends. Thanks to the treachery of Quickstep we know this. You will be well advised to take the way I have shown you."

"I think Bede's right. We should take the safer route," Shortpaws piped up. Twitchwhisker had forgotten all about Shortpaws. He turned to his small companion.

"We?" Twitchwhisker asked. "Who said you were coming along?"

Shortpaws looked shocked by the harshness of Twitchwhisker's reply. "I thought . . ."

"Then you thought wrongly," Twitchwhisker snapped before Shortpaws could finish. "I must do this alone."

Shortpaws looked imploringly at Bede.

"I must agree with Twitchwhisker," the old mouse said. "Your presence would only serve to double the folly of this endeavour."

Shortpaws began to say something, but the words choked in his throat. He stood before them his eyes glistenening with tears and then suddenly, before either Twitchwhisker or Bede could say anything further, he turned away and scurried out of Bede's chamber.

Twitchwhisker called after him.

"Let him go," said Bede. "You will only make matters worse."

"I just wanted to tell him that I had to go alone because I didn't want him to be hurt."

"I understand," replied Bede, "and he shall too. Should you fail to return I will talk to him."

"I shall return. I do not intend to fail," Twitchwhisker said defiantly.

"We shall see," Bede replied. "No mouse knows his fate. I advise caution, Twitchwhisker, and you would

do well to heed me.

"I will. I promise," said Twitchwhisker.

"I doubt that," said Bede. "Your head is full of dreams, mouseling, dreams of glory and bright valour. The same dreams could prove to be your undoing. Remember you are mouse-kind not human born."

Twitchwhisker forced a laugh at Bede's dark, warning words. "We can discuss my dreams when I return," he said with great bravado and with that he took his leave and went off to prepare for his forthcoming adventure.

At the door of her chamber, Morgana turned to Sir Modred who had escorted her back from the feast.

"Thank you, Sir Knight," she said sweetly. "You may leave me here and attend to your business."

Modred gallantly bowed and kissed her hand. "Fear not, madam," he replied. "All shall be taken care of. Come the dawn you shall be queen."

A few moments later Modred was on his way to keep his appointment with Bandalf and Cedric. When he reached their hiding place he knocked three times, once sharply and then twice softly. The door creaked open and Modred slipped in. "All is ready," he whispered. "The wine is on its way to the guards."

"How long must we wait?" Bandalf asked. He was impatient to get on with the job. Cedric said nothing. He sat silently in a corner of the room sharpening his knife, the one which would soon end the king's life.

"An hour will see them sleeping soundly," Modred replied. "Wait until the watch calls from the gatehouse and then you may make your move. I trust you remember the way to Arthur's chamber?"

"Your directions are engraved on my memory, sir," said Bandalf. "We shall not lose our way. I trust you have the rest of our gold."

"Do not worry," said Modred, "you shall have payment in full when you take your leave. It will be awaiting you when you have completed your task."

Bandalf smiled at the thought of the gold, not knowing that Modred's 'payment in full' would

   72

actually be a score of arrows to cut them down as they left Camelot. "Then you may leave the rest to us, sir," Bandalf assured Modred. "And should you require our services in the future we should only be too honoured to serve."

"We shall see," Modred replied and he left.

Sir Modred went directly to the chamber of a fellow knight, Sir Bors, with whom he had earlier arranged a friendly game of dice. Sir Bors loved gambling — unfortunately he rarely won — but this time he would. Modred was determined to see to that. Modred would make sure that Sir Bors would win heavily, so heavily in fact that he would not be able to contain his joy and all Camelot would know the following day. They would also know that Modred had spent the early hours in the company of Sir Bors and thus Modred would be completely above suspicion when Arthur's body was discovered.

It was the final touch to what he considered to be a perfect plan and Modred was justly proud of it. Apart from Morgana who would there be to say that he had a part in the foul deed? Bandalf and Cedric would die and if his guards were asked why they were present just as the assassins made their escape they would answer that Modred had instructed them to be constantly vigilant for the king's safety and the whole court would applaud his concern. It was perfect. He knocked on Sir Bors' chamber door and was greeted by the stout, beaming knight.

"Ah, Sir Modred — at last. I have been waiting. I must warn you I feel very lucky. Have you brought a good purse with you?"

"Indeed, Sir Bors," Modred smiled. "A purseful for the taking."

Perfect.

In the now deserted Great Hall the last of the candles which had blazed as bright as constellations during the feast flickered and one by one went out. Darkness invaded the scene, casting deep shadows everywhere. The remains of the feast lay on the long tables. Mountains of food were now mountains of scraps, food for the pigs when the morning came, a rich prize for scavengers.

All was as quiet as a graveyard and amongst the shadows, hidden, waiting for the expected hordes of mice lay the cats of Camelot. As soon as the feast ended and human-kind had gone to their beds the cats came on Wolfbane's orders and took up their positions. There were ten cats in all, including Wolfbane; a motley bunch of feline ferocity waiting for their victims to walk into the trap set for them. Now almost an hour had passed and nothing stirred. Where were the mice? Why had they not yet come, the cats began to wonder?

"The others grow restless, Wolfbane," said Tornear. "How much longer shall we wait?"

Wolfbane looked squarely at his lieutenant. "Until I decide otherwise," he growled. Wolfbane was angry. His plan to massacre the mice had failed and Wolfbane did not like to fail. He knew what had happened. He knew where the blame lay. The two spies in the

Armoury had managed to return and reveal the plot. The thought of the two mice made him unsheathe a pawful of claws. He would have them eventually! But first he had to try and salvage something out of the shambles of his plan. "Grimclaw!" he hissed through the darkness.

Grimclaw, a rough-haired grey tabby, padded across to his leader.

"Take three of the others and prowl from the Armoury to the wine-cellars. Tornear, you shall take the remainder and make for the kitchens."

"And what of you?" Tornear ventured to ask.

"I shall go alone," Wolfbane replied. "I have the strangest feeling that my presence will be required elsewhere."

As soon as the others left to do his bidding, Wolfbane set out himself, gliding off through the shadows, melting into the darkness like a ghost.

Unknown to Wolfbane and the Camelot cats their departure did not go unnoticed. As they went their separate ways, the scout-mice Bede had instructed to keep watch, scurried back to inform him that the cats were on their way. The message reached him at one of the large pantries next to the kitchen where he was personally supervising the removal of supplies. In the past such a raid would have been unthinkable. Wolfbane usually kept the pantries well guarded, but knowing that the cats were occupied in the Great Hall, Bede had decided on a bold and direct raid.

He had expected the message to come sooner than it had. With its coming he ordered the last of the mice to leave immediately.

"Hurry along now," he commanded. "Time is short."

There was no fuss or bother, no panic whatsoever. Bede had everything under control. Almost two whole cheeses had been removed and now it was time to go. As the last mouse left the pantry with the haul, Bede checked that no one was left behind and then quickly followed.

The raiding party soon reached the safety of the colony. Bede organized the storing of the cheese and ordered an immediate ration to be given out. There was great rejoicing. When the cheese had been distributed and after making his report to Amos, Bede went to look for Twitchwhisker, hoping that the young mouse had not yet set off. Enquiring about his whereabouts he was told that Twitchwhisker had been

77

seen earlier leaving the colony. Bede's informant added that he had also seen Shortpaws leaving.

"I think he was following Twitchwhisker," the mouse told Bede.

Bede thanked him and returned to his chamber. He felt very tired now and snuggled down for a nap. "Foolish mice," he muttered as his old eyes closed. "Foolish young mice." There was nothing he could do now except wait . . . and see if fortune on this occasion would favour the brave.

It was as Twitchwhisker reached the staircase which led to the North Tower that he realized he was being followed. He stopped and listened. Yes, there it was again. A definite pitter-pat of pawsteps. It was not cat-kind he was certain of that. Cat-kind made no noise. Who or what could it be? He decided to take cover and find out. A nearby tapestry provided him with a hiding place. The sounds grew closer. Pitter-pat. Pitter-pat. Whoever, or whatever, followed him, was now almost upon him. He peeked cautiously out. He saw his follower approaching breathlessly out of the corridor's gloom. Well, would you believe it! He leapt out from his hiding place.

"What are you doing here?" he stormed angrily at Shortpaws.

Shortpaws jumped into the air, frightened by Twitchwhisker's sudden appearance.

"Well!" demanded Twitchwhisker. "I asked you a question."

"Please don't shout, Twitch," Shortpaws replied.

"Shout! I feel like giving you a good nipping. You deserve no less. I told you that I had to do this alone. When will you ever learn? You must go back immediately."

"Go back?" Shortpaws squeaked. "By myself?"

"You came by yourself," said Twitchwhisker.

"Not so. I came with you. I had you in my sights all the time," Shortpaws explained. "Please don't send me back, Twitch. Let me come with you. I won't be a burden I promise."

Twitchwhisker clicked his teeth together as mice often do when they are angry. Against his better judgement he agreed to allow his friend along.

"At least I'll be able to keep my eyes on you. Now let us go. We have wasted too much time already."

Shortpaws breathed a sigh of relief. "Oh thank you, Twitch. I promise to do everything you say."

"I told you not to come," Twitchwhisker reminded him.

"That was different," Shortpaws replied happily.

From the battlements the watchman sang out that all was well and continued on his way. It began to snow once again. The big flakes swirled around like mad insects, blown by the wind which swept coldly from the North.

In the courtyard below a door creaked open. The head of Bandalf appeared. He looked around and seeing that the way was clear called quietly to Cedric and together they stealthily made their way across the courtyard towards the Great Hall . . .

. . . "Are you sure this is the North Tower?" Shortpaws asked as Twitchwhisker pulled him up another flight of steps.

"If you ask me that again I'll drop you," Twitchwhisker replied. "Of course it's the North Tower. Now climb more and talk less . . ."

★

On soft, silent, deadly paws Wolfbane padded along the dark passages of Camelot. He sniffed the air as he prowled . . . mice somewhere — there were mice somewhere . . . some had passed this way lately . . .

★

"A six! A six!" Sir Bors shouted with delight as the dice tumbled. "That's another gold piece, Modred."

Sir Modred pushed another coin across to Sir Bors. "You are incredibly lucky, Sir Bors."

"Long overdue," observed the stout knight. "Another throw, Sir Modred? Perhaps you shall win this time."

Modred picked up the dice and smiled pleasantly at his companion. "Indeed, Sir Bors, sometimes you have to lose in order to later win . . ."

★

Beneath black sheets Morgana slept soundly and dreamt. She was seated regally on Arthur's throne and above her head, hands were poised to place the crown. She felt its heavy weight descend and heard the voices around her shout, "Hail Morgana! Hail Morgana! Long live Queen Morgana!"

★

. . . on and on went Wolfbane with his head hung low, moving panther-like through the darkness . . .

★

Outside King Arthur's chamber the second guard slid slowly to the floor and joined his companion. He hiccuped once and burbled happily before falling fast asleep . . .

★

. . . across the Great Hall towards the North Tower slipped two fleeting shadows. Bandalf and Cedric were halfway to their destination . . .

★

. . ."You lose again, Sir Modred," chortled Sir Bors. He scooped up the dice. "Another game?" he asked hopefully.

Modred nodded. "My throw I believe," he said . . .

★

. . . it was like scaling a mountain. Up one step and then the next, huffing and puffing, the two tiny adventurers climbed the last few steps.

"Not far now," panted Twitchwhisker. "We're almost there."

★

Outside the snow continued to fall. Snow upon snow, white upon white, softness upon softness. Everything looked so peaceful, so calm and Christmassy. Who would have suspected that Death was stalking the corridors so dark at that moment? Who would have imagined the dreadful deed which was taking place? Who would have thought that the life of good King Arthur hung that moment by a thread, a thread in the hands, nay in the paws of two small mice?

Chapter Twelve
Desperate Measures

At the end of the short corridor leading from the top of the stairs stood the doorway to King Arthur's chamber. Outside it lay the two guards, slumped forward like oversized rag-dolls.

"Are they dead?" Shortpaws whispered. He hung behind Twitchwhisker, somewhat fearful of approaching any further.

"Of course not. They're asleep. Modred had wine sent to them which caused them to sleep. Come along. Don't be afraid. They won't wake up."

Twitchwhisker moved confidently towards the two slumbering figures, a mouse David approaching two Goliaths. Cautiously Shortpaws followed ready to retreat at the slightest hint of danger. As he neared the foot of the nearest guard the man grunted in his drugged sleep and twitched. Within seconds Shortpaws was back at the top of the stairs.

"Come back here at once!" Twitchwhisker ordered.

Full of shame, Shortpaws sidled back to his friend's side. "He moved," the tiny mouse whispered trying to justify his rapid retreat.

"And so do you when you're asleep. You toss and turn repeatedly," Twitchwhisker hissed. "Believe me, they are asleep. Do you want me to prove it to you? Say the word and I shall nip him for you."

"No . . o . . o . . oo!" squeaked Shortpaws. "I believe you!"

"Then come. Time is wasting. For all we know

those two villains are already inside." As if to make his point Twitchwhisker laid his ear to the door of the chamber and listened intently for a few moments.

"Can you hear anything?"

"Someone snoring. The king I should think," Twitchwhisker answered. "I can't hear anything else. I think we're in time. The problem now is how to get in. I can't see a crack anywhere."

He examined the door closely. Many of the doors in Camelot were old and worn, but as luck would have it the king's door was a perfect fit. There was no way in, not even for a mouse. The door towered above him. It might as well have been a sheer mountain face. How he wished at that moment that he was as tall as humankind. Then the door would be no problem whatsoever. He would simply open the door and wake the king. He saw himself.

"Your Majesty! Wake up! Wake up! Your life is in danger."

"And who, sir, are you?" the king would ask.

"Your humble servant, sire. Here to save your life."

"My life? What do you mean?"

"There is no time to waste, sire. Two villains are on their way at this very moment to take your life. Modred has paid them in gold."

"Modred!" The king's eyes would narrow at the mention of that traitor's name. And then suddenly, before anything further could be done the two villains would appear at the door of the chamber. The king would toss him a sword and he would leap into action. There would be a clash of steel. Sparks would fly and with justice strengthening his arm and courage his armour he would

84

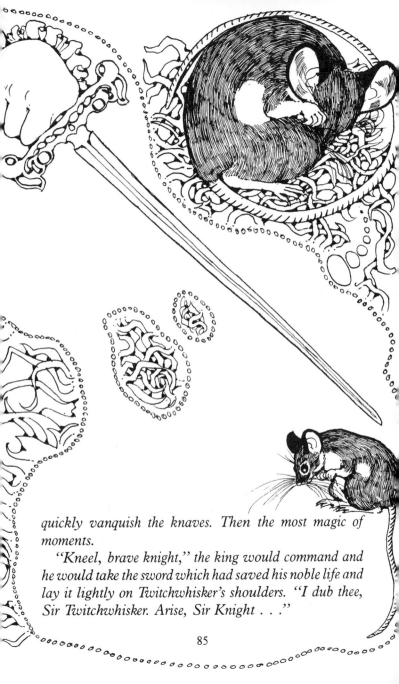

quickly vanquish the knaves. Then the most magic of moments.

"Kneel, brave knight," the king would command and he would take the sword which had saved his noble life and lay it lightly on Twitchwhisker's shoulders. "I dub thee, Sir Twitchwhisker. Arise, Sir Knight . . ."

85

". . . night." Shortpaw's tremulous voice interrupted the ceremony. The dream dissolved.

"What?" Twitchwhisker asked.

"I said what are we going to do? We can't stop here all night."

"I don't intend we shall," Twitchwhisker replied.

His mind worked feverishly. It was impossible to get into the king's chamber . . . so . . . so . . . yes, that was it! They could not get to the king so he must come to them! They must rouse him. But how? How? His eyes swept around the corridor. Nearby stood a suit of armour. That would make a fine crash if they could push it over. Twitchwhisker considered the task and the effort required. No, it was too much for two small mice. Even a hundred mice would find it difficult. Something else . . . something else. The only other object in the corridor was a heavy wooden chandelier which hung high above them, holding a dozen or so burning candles. It was suspended by a rope which passed over a small pulley along the ceiling and over another pulley where it then passed down to a metal ring to which it was secured. The ring itself was secured in the wall near the chamber door. Twitchwhisker immediately saw the opportunity which presented itself. Yes! It was their only chance. If they could bring the chandelier down surely that would rouse the king.

Twitchwhisker judged distances. The ring and thus the rope were reachable. He would have to climb onto the head of the nearest guard and leap for the rope. There was not a moment to lose . . .

"Go to the top of the stairs and keep watch," he ordered Shortpaws.

"What are you going to . . . ?"

"Don't ask!" Twitchwhisker snapped. "Every moment is vital. Squeak out if you hear anyone coming."

Shortpaws obeyed and took up his position at the head of the stairs.

Twitchwhisker leapt into action. He quickly scaled the mountain of slumbering flesh and in a trice was on a shoulder. Now for the summit. He took a pawhold in an ear and hauled himself up to the helmet. Gripping the rim of the helmet tightly he strained every muscle and pushing with his hind legs shimmied his way to the curved summit. Success! Twitchwhisker breathed a sigh of relief. So far so good and now for the most difficult part! He steadied himself.

The rope was tantalizingly near, but still far enough away for him to pause and consider before he attempted to bridge the gap which separated them. He would have to throw himself three times his own length; not impossible but nevertheless long enough to be dangerous. If he missed, the plunge down could result in a broken leg. For a moment Twitchwhisker hesitated. Then he dismissed all consequences from his mind. It was for the king. What greater glory could anyone ask? He silently summoned his courage and his strength. Mouse-muscles coiled themselves. Ears sloped backwards and without further ado, Twitchwhisker hurled himself outwards and upwards towards the rope.

It was a split-second movement. He was a blur of fur. Tiny paws grasped at the rough surface of the rope. One slipped, but one held. Held tight.

"Don't fall, Twitch!" he heard Shortpaw's squeak.

Twitchwhisker had no intention of falling. With the rope gripped firmly in one paw he began to pull himself upwards, swinging his body.

"I told you to keep watch!" he stormed. "Do so!"

He hauled himself up to safety and found himself perched on the ring and the knot which held the rope secure. He rested for another moment.

"Hear anything?" he squeaked breathlessly.

"Nothing," Shortpaws replied.

Twitchwhisker caught his breath. There was still time then. Fortune was still smiling upon them. Now only the rope stood between the king's safety and the villains. He looked at the knot. Whoever had tied it had made sure that it would not slip. He tugged at it. No, that would not do. It would not budge. There was only one thing for it. He would have to gnaw his way through the rope and hope that he could complete his task before Modred's murderous duo came. Undaunted and filled with resolve to save the king he attacked the rope. The twisted strands of fibre began to separate under the gnawing assault. Without pause Twitchwhisker gnawed. He gnawed and gnawed until his jaws ached. A life depended upon his sharp teeth. A king's life. A noble life. He held that thought in his mind and shut out anything else, allowing nothing to distract him.

"Twitch! I can hear something."

Shortpaw's warning served to redouble his efforts. His teeth flashed. Fibres parted. How far through was he? A third? Yes, at least a third. Press on! Press on!

"Twitch! They're here. I'm sure it's them," Shortpaw's frantic voice squeaked. He scuttled back. "It's too late! Too late! Jump for it."

Twitchwhisker paid no heed to Shortpaw's dire words. His teeth continued to flash as he tore at the rough fibres. His jaws ached. His teeth felt blunted and sore yet still he continued.

Shortpaws took cover behind the nearest guard. "Jump, Twitch, before it's too late and you are caught!" he begged.

"Never," Twitch gasped. "Hide yourself."

89

Shortpaws needed no further persuasion.

At the top of the stairs a face with weasel-bright eyes peered cautiously around the corner. It smiled at the scene before it. Above it another, larger head appeared.

Bandalf and Cedric had arrived.

Like two wolves they padded towards the door. Shortpaws held his breath. Twitchwhisker slipped behind the knot and continued his gnawing. Retreat was out of the question. With luck they would not see him.

Bandalf reached down and lifted the eyelids of one of the guards. "Sleeping like a babe," he whispered to Cedric.

Cedric smiled monstrously.

Bandalf unsheathed a small dagger and his companion followed his example.

Twitchwhisker's heart pounded. The weapons glinted in the candlelight. Now desperation gripped him. He gnawed for all he was worth. Strand after strand parted.

Bandalf silently opened the door. There was death in his eyes. Death in his hand. He moved forward.

Too late! I'm too late! Twitchwhisker moaned silently. Dread filled his tiny heart. The king was lost!

At that moment, as the two men edged their way into the chamber, Fate took a hand in the proceedings. The weight of the chandelier proved too much for the weakened rope to bear. Twitchwhisker's downcast heart leapt with delight as the strands began to break by themselves. The rope found a voice. It groaned. It pinged. It pinged and groaned.

Twitch stood back. "Break! Break!" he called to the rope.

The squeaks and the groan of the rope alerted Cedric. He glanced over his shoulder. His slow brain tried to comprehend the situation. He saw Twitchwhisker. Mouse? Mouse?? Rope? Rope??? Rope breaking? What to do? So many things to think of at once. He tapped Bandalf urgently on the shoulder. Bandalf would know what to do.

Bandalf whirled around as the last few strands of the rope gave way under the strain. Instantly he saw the danger and leapt silently to catch the end of the rope, but even Bandalf's lightning reflexes were not fast enough.

The tattered end slipped through his fingers and with an ear-shattering crash the chandelier fell to the stone floor!

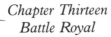

Chapter Thirteen
Battle Royal

The scene which immediately followed remained engraved in the memory of Twitchwhisker for the rest of his days. Oft had he heard the stories of combat told by the knights as they sat at the Round Table, but never in his wildest imagination did he ever think that he would witness one at such close quarters.

The falling of the chandelier had the precise effect which Twitchwhisker had hoped for. The king was roused from his slumber. Roused do I say? He leapt up as if struck by lightning. At his bedside stood his sword, Excalibur. In the wink of an eye it was out of its scabbard and King Arthur was on his feet ready for the fray.

"What ho!" he roared. "What's afoot? What mischief!"

He strode forward in his nightshirt, sword in hand, towards the open chamber door. He saw the two guards slumped on the floor and the two villains between them. "Aha!" he exclaimed. A fierce light was in his eyes. The light of a warrior prepared for battle.

"Get him!" Bandalf snarled to his massive companion.

Cedric launched himself with a ferocious roar, his dagger at the ready. On he rushed straight at the king, who anticipating the charge swiftly side-stepped. Cedric was unable to stop himself and disappeared into the chamber propelled with a flat, rump-stinging stroke from the king's sword.

Arthur whirled around to face Bandalf. Steel clashed with steel. King Arthur flung the villain from him and followed quickly with a slashing stroke which drove Bandalf backwards in search of safety.

Cedric emerged from the chamber and joined the fray again. The king was forced to retreat and backed into a corner. He slashed at the two assailants keeping them at bay as a stag keeps wolves at bay with his sharp antlers. Despite the dangers, Twitchwhisker stood his ground. Several times during the fight he was almost brushed from his perch as the battling humans drew

close. It was only when the king's sword swung
dangerously close and chippings of stone showered
upon him that he decided to move. He threw himself
down onto the guard and scrambled down to join
Shortpaws. Shortpaws was trembling with fear. The
noise of battle was deafening. Cut and thrust. Slash
and stab. Valiantly the king fought. He was a match for
the two villains. Time and time again he drove them
back. Twitchwhisker had never seen such bravery. At
times he could not stop himself and called out, "Have
at him, sire! That's it. Deal with the dogs!"

He was almost disappointed when rescue for the king came. A handful of his valiant knights appeared at the top of the stairs and rushed in to aid their liege lord. Twitchwhisker recognized the rescuers. Sir Lancelot! Sir Gawain and Sir Galahad!

Within minutes they had overwhelmed Bandalf and Cedric and disarmed them. Guards arrived and the two villains were placed in their custody. Before they were led away the king asked why they sought to kill him.

"Perhaps this is the answer, sire," said Sir Lancelot. He pulled from Bandalf's jerkin the money pouch filled with Modred's gold. "I know of few ruffians who honestly possess such wealth."

"So," the king said to Bandalf, "a goodly price for a king's life."

"And more to come," Bandalf sneered.

"Even better," the king answered boldly. "How unfortunate for you that you shall not collect the remainder. Take them away. I shall question them some more, shortly."

"Yes, sire." The captain of the guard bowed and led the prisoners away.

"Lancelot, you will stay with me whilst I dress. The rest of you may go. I am indebted to you for hastening so speedily to my aid."

The corridor emptied and the king with Lancelot in attendance returned to his chamber and dressed.

"A close encounter, sire," Sir Lancelot observed as he helped King Arthur to dress. "Did the miscreants rouse thee?"

"Most curious is that, Lancelot," the king replied.

"See yonder chandelier. To it I owe my life, brave knight. I know not why, but from my slumber by its falling was I roused."

The king stepped into the corridor and examined the rope. "Observe how it looks. What thinkest thou? An accident? A weakness in the twining perhaps?"

"Most like, sire," answered Lancelot. "It is too ragged for a knife's attention. But whatsoever caused it, to it we owe our fortune that you still live."

"Amen to that!" the king laughed. "Now come, sirrah. Let us go and discover what yon two wretches have disclosed."

Lancelot and the king left the chamber, not knowing that they left behind them the true cause of the 'accident' which had saved the royal life.

Twitchwhisker and Shortpaws emerged from their hiding place. Shortpaws breathed a sigh of relief and declared that he was glad that it was over and done with. "I thought they'd never leave," he said.

"Wasn't it fantastic!" Twitchwhisker squeaked. His eyes were shining with happiness. "Did you see the king fight? Wasn't he noble! Wasn't he brave! Did you see how he tore into those two villains? I've never seen anything like it before."

He leapt around acrobatically slashing and stabbing at imaginary assailants. "What wouldn't I give to be a knight! How I'd love to have been at his side." He dealt a mortal blow to one of his invisible attackers. "Die craven dog!" he snarled withdrawing his make-believe sword. A groan interrupted his performance. One of the guards stirred.

"Twitch! We must away!" Shortpaws squeaked.

Twitchwhisker snorted indignantly. He sheathed his sword with bravado. "Let us go then," he said. "Our work is finished here."

Shortpaws scampered after his friend and they made their way to the stairs before the guards could regain consciousness. Descending the stairs was much easier than the ascent. In no time at all they were at the bottom, ready to start their journey back to the colony. Twitchwhisker considered which way to go.

"Perhaps we should return the way we came," Shortpaws said.

"Trust you," Twitchwhisker replied. "Safety-first Shortpaws. No, we shall go through the Great Hall. We might see the king. I wonder if Modred has been arrested yet?"

Shortpaws began to protest, reminding Twitchwhisker of Bede's earlier warning, but Twitchwhisker would not hear any argument and led the way to the hall before Shortpaws could finish.

Chapter Fourteen
The Final Meeting

There had been another witness to the events which took place outside the king's chamber. Following the trail of Twitchwhisker and Shortpaws, Wolfbane had found himself climbing the staircase which spiralled up the tall North Tower. He arrived at the top as the fight between the king and his assailants began and decided immediately that he would pursue his prey no further. He made a silent retreat down the stairs only just in time to avoid the knights dashing to the rescue of His Majesty.

But Wolfbane was not a cat to be deterred easily. The mice had climbed the tower and eventually they would have to descend. He would wait. Everything comes to those who wait. It was a question of patience and Wolfbane had lots of patience. He decided that he would await their return in the Great Hall from whence he'd come. There was a chance of course that they would return by a different route and yet he sensed that his choice was the right one.

Whilst he awaited the mice in the Great Hall, Wolfbane met Tornear and his cronies drifting back from their search. Wolfbane could tell by their faces that they had been unsuccessful. When asked by his lieutenant what they should do next, Wolfbane dismissed them and ordered that the other patrol party led by Grimclaw be told of his decision.

"There will be another day," he promised them. He

watched the cats slink away to their resting places for the night.

Wolfbane settled himself, choosing a shadowy alcove near the exit to the kitchens below. Everything comes to those who wait and Wolfbane did not have long to wait. He saw the two mice approaching long before they saw him. They entered from the corridor which led from the North Tower. Wolfbane flattened himself and watched them approach. As he had suspected all along they were the same two who had thwarted him twice before. The two spies from the Armoury. The very same mice who had caused him so much trouble. But now he would take his revenge. This time they would not escape him. Come little fools, he purred to himself, Wolfbane awaits you.

Knowing not what lay in wait for them, Twitchwhisker and Shortpaws scuttled through the shadows. They came like lambs to the slaughter. Wolfbane waited until they were almost upon him before he stepped out and revealed his presence.

It was always a delicious moment. That first moment when the eyes of his victims filled with terror as they realized that death was only a pawslength away. How wide their eyes grew! How wide with terror were the eyes of these two who stood before him now.

"Greetings, mouselings," he purred. "Whither goest thou?" An evil smile spread slowly across his feline features. "What, no reply? Are we not old friends? Our paths have crossed before have they not? Surely you remember?"

For a moment neither of the mice spoke. Then the larger one spoke up at last. "I think perhaps you are mistaken," he replied very politely. "I do not remember meeting before. If we had I would be sure to remember."

Wolfbane laughed softly. "And I say that it is *you* who are mistaken, mouseling. Met we most certainly have. On two occasions before to be exact. You were in the Armoury and in the chamber of my mistress."

The larger mouse looked at his companion as if to say 'Do you know what he means?'

This irritated Wolfbane. "Come now, mouselings. Do not play games with me. You know of what I speak. Your meddling has caused me great distress; great distress indeed and now I'm afraid you must pay the price."

There was something quite admirable in the way the mouse replied, Wolfbane thought. Here he was, moments away from oblivion, and he had the nerve to be calm. "Price? What price?"

"Oh, I think you know," Wolfbane purred silkily. "Even a mouse is not so stupid. No — do not move. Do you wish to hasten your fate?"

He took one step forward and noted with satisfaction how they shrank back. That was what Wolfbane liked to see. Fear. Absolute fear. It was what he lived for. He was Wolfbane, the terror of Camelot. How he enjoyed seeing things tremble in his presence!

Twitchwhisker saw the gloating gleam in Wolfbane's eyes. He knew that if he and Shortpaws were to escape from the doom promised they would have to act. And this was the moment, whilst Wolfbane was congratulating himself. Without any warning he moved and sent Shortpaws staggering backwards,

propelled by a hefty push. "Run!" he shouted.

Wolfbane pounced but the mice were no longer where they were a second before. "So you wish to play," he called out to the shadows.

Wolfbane pricked up his ears. His eyes searched the darkness. He padded silently forward. Aha! There behind a table leg. A thin tail quivering like a blade of grass in the wind. As silently as a thought moved Wolfbane. Reaching out a paw he clamped the tail to the cold stone floor. The squeak of terror which followed was music to his ears.

"Well, well," whispered Wolfbane. "What have we here?" The owner of the tail struggled and tried to escape. Wolfbane applied more pressure. "Do not struggle little one," he advised. "Accept your fate. I shall be kind and make your ending swift." He smiled

at the trapped Shortpaws.

A moment later the smile had vanished from his face and the kind, soft voice was replaced by a yowl of pain. Sticking in his hind leg was a sharp, chicken bone. It was wielded by Twitchwhisker! He held it like a spear and thrust as hard as he could regardless of his own safety. Wolfbane immediately loosened his hold on Shortpaws and turned to face his tiny tormentor. His eyes blazed with anger.

"Upstart mouseling, for that there will be no mercy. No swift ending for you! You shall feel my claws. Prepare yourself for a thousand cuts!" he hissed. Out flicked a paw. Twitchwhisker parried the blow with his spear. He staggered backwards. Another paw flicked out. Again it was parried and again he was driven back.

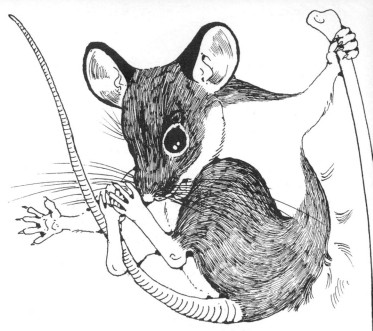

"You fight bravely, mouseling," Wolfbane said. "But your puny weapon will not save you." He slashed out. Razor-sharp claws brushed mouse-fur and raked the skin beneath.

Twitchwhisker squealed shrilly in pain.

"The first of many, mouseling. You should learn to mind your own business. Why did you not escape whilst you had the chance?"

"You would not understand," Twitchwhisker replied bravely. He was driven further back. Wolfbane loomed large above him. Twitchwhisker could feel and smell his hot beath. It was the smell of death.

"You are tiring, mouseling," Wolfbane said. "I can see it in your eyes. Why bother to resist further? Lay down your weapon. I shall relent and make your going swift. I will forgive your impudence in attacking me."

There was something almost soothing in the words of Wolfbane and the blazing amber eyes promised sleep beyond pain. They were moons, amber moons which hypnotized, growing larger, larger . . .

Twitchwhisker was rooted to the spot. His legs seemed unable to move. He willed them to move, but they would not. Death was a whisker away. He tried to hold himself up but, weakened by Wolfbane's attack, faint-headed and dizzy from loss of blood his legs folded beneath him. It was the end and he knew it.

''That's the way, little one. Soon you shall rest for eternity.''

The toothful jaws yawned open and the black chasm of Wolfbane's throat beckoned. With one last despairing act of defiance Twitchwhisker raised the chicken-bone spear. He waited, eyes closed, for the sharp fangs to sink into his small body.

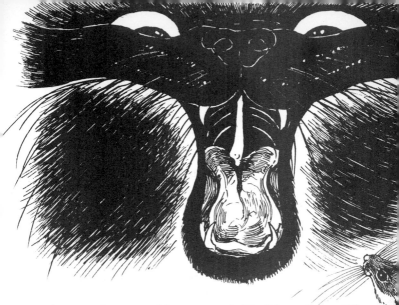

An eternity passed in a second. He felt nothing. Was he dead? Was this Death? He opened his eyes. No, he was not dead. What was Wolfbane doing? The terrible cat was clawing at his throat. It was then that Twitchwhisker realized what must have happened. As the jaws were about to close on him they had closed instead on the upraised bone which had become jammed in the open mouth. Wolfbane could not open his jaws any further and he could not close them. The pain was terrible. The pain was excruciating. He tried to dislodge the bone. It would not move and each time he touched it the pain was unbearable. The Great Hall echoed with his high-pitched yowls of agony.

Forgotten by Wolfbane, Twitchwhisker seized his opportunity to escape. He ran for the stairs which led down to the kitchens.

"Twitch!" Shortpaws scuttled towards him out of the darkness. "Are you badly hurt?" He touched

Twitchwhisker's shoulder. Warm, slippery redness stained his paw. "You're bleeding!" he squeaked.

"A scratch. Nothing more," Twitch replied though he felt quite some pain.

Wolfbane yowled once again. Shortpaws jumped in fright.

"Don't worry," Twitchwhisker assured him. "He will not harm us any more. He is otherwise engaged. See, there he goes now. I think it will be a long time before he will bother a mouse again."

They saw Wolfbane crawling away, yowling and mewing piteously as he went.

"Serves him right," Shortpaws said. "Wait until we tell the others how we defeated Wolfbane. Go on you black devil! Slink away!"

"How *we* defeated Wolfbane?" Twitchwhisker looked reprovingly at his suddenly bold friend. "Where were *you* when he was about to make a meal of me?"

"Oh, I knew you would be all right. Honest, Twitch! I was ready to have at him and give him a good nipping."

"I bet you were," said Twitchwhisker.

"I was — honestly!" Shortpaws replied indignantly.

"I know," said Twitchwhisker, "I was teasing you. Let us go. We've done enough for one day I believe. Onward mice!"

"Onward!" chimed Shortpaws and together the two tiny adventurers trooped off merrily to return to their own kind; two adventurers who by their daring and extraordinary courage had saved the life of a king and defeated their greatest enemy along the way.

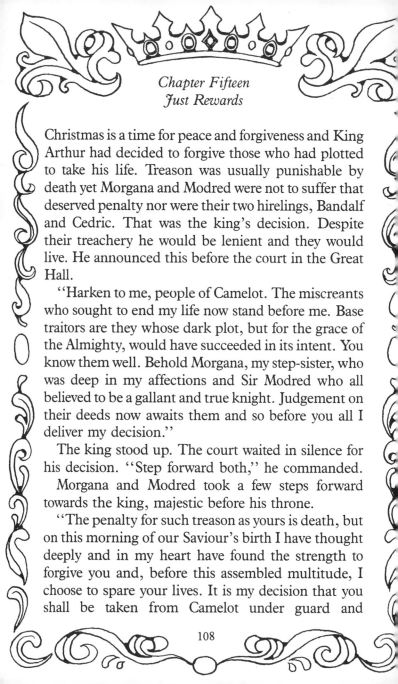

Chapter Fifteen
Just Rewards

Christmas is a time for peace and forgiveness and King Arthur had decided to forgive those who had plotted to take his life. Treason was usually punishable by death yet Morgana and Modred were not to suffer that deserved penalty nor were their two hirelings, Bandalf and Cedric. That was the king's decision. Despite their treachery he would be lenient and they would live. He announced this before the court in the Great Hall.

"Harken to me, people of Camelot. The miscreants who sought to end my life now stand before me. Base traitors are they whose dark plot, but for the grace of the Almighty, would have succeeded in its intent. You know them well. Behold Morgana, my step-sister, who was deep in my affections and Sir Modred who all believed to be a gallant and true knight. Judgement on their deeds now awaits them and so before you all I deliver my decision."

The king stood up. The court waited in silence for his decision. "Step forward both," he commanded.

Morgana and Modred took a few steps forward towards the king, majestic before his throne.

"The penalty for such treason as yours is death, but on this morning of our Saviour's birth I have thought deeply and in my heart have found the strength to forgive you and, before this assembled multitude, I choose to spare your lives. It is my decision that you shall be taken from Camelot under guard and conducted to the borders of my kingdom from whence you shall begin your exile. Yes, exile is your punishment. Never again are you allowed to set foot in this land. Do so at your own peril. Should you choose to return you shall suffer just punishment for your crimes. As for your unfortunate partners in crime — bring them forward!''

Bandalf and Cedric were led forward. Their legs were shackled and their hands manacled. The king drew himself erect and addressed them.

''To you also I extend the hand of mercy. Your lust for gold has led you to this end and you deserve the full measure of justice. Instead, likewise you shall be driven from my kingdom. Return and the fate promised to my sister and this errant knight awaits you also.''

Arthur turned to the guards who surrounded the four and addressed the captain. ''Into your charge I place them. Allow them to gather their personal possessions and what they shall require for their journey. After which you shall conduct them from my kingdom.''

As the guards stepped forward to lead the new exiles away, Morgana, with a defiant toss of her head, approached the king. The captain of the guard reached out to draw her back.

''No, leave her be. I think she has something to say to me.''

Morgana did have something to say.

''Brother, before I leave I would thank you for your mercy. As ever you have shown the true quality of kingship and in return I would tell you that never will

109

your kindness be forgotten. We shall think long on your words and I promise that it will eventually be repaid in full.''

No one in the hall that morning doubted what Morgana meant. Though her words were soft and full of sincerity they knew that Morgana meant the exact opposite of what she said. In her voice was the promise of revenge and her eyes could not conceal the hatred she had for her step-brother. She said nothing more. Morgana bowed and turned away to be followed by her companions in crime and their escort.

110

As their footsteps died away King Arthur raised his hands to quieten the court for there were those amongst the king's loyal followers who doubted the wisdom of his decision. A hush descended on the assembly.

"And now dear friends," the king began, replacing the solemn expression on his noble features with a ready smile, "let us turn to lighter matters. Banish from your thoughts the dark deeds now past. Pray be joyful on this Christmas morn. Let us continue with the festivities. Tonight we will feast again and I beg you make these old stone walls ring with the sounds of our merriment!"

His words were greeted with great approval by all and thus with a triumphant fanfare of trumpets, accompanied by his courtiers the king left the Great Hall.

As soon as he departed orders were quickly issued by the Chief Steward of Camelot and the preparations for the feast began.

Once again in the kitchens below the Great Hall there were scenes of furious activity as the kitchen staff made ready. Hustle and bustle, clatter and clamour! It was business as usual . . .

Things had also returned to normal in the world of Camelot mice. After their final encounter with Wolfbane, Twitchwhisker and Shortpaws returned safely to the colony. Bede was waiting for them and welcomed them warmly. He led them to his chamber where he had refreshments for them. They tucked in gladly. Their adventures had given them a good appetite. As they ate, they told Bede about their

narrow squeak in the North Tower and their even
narrower squeak in the Great Hall.

"So you saved the life of a human king?"

"You could say we had a paw in it," Twitchwhisker
replied modestly.

"A paw in it!" Shortpaws squeaked up. "You saved
the king's life almost single-handedly."

"You did your bit. I couldn't have done it alone," Twitchwhisker told him.

Shortpaws was about to protest and say that he hadn't done anything really when Bede intervened.

"Enough! — you are both heroes. Due to your efforts the human king lives on. Nevertheless it was still foolish of you. I hope that you have tasted enough danger for a while and are prepared to return to your duties. I cannot promise you the excitement you have apparently grown so used to, though I daresay you will find your fair share in the near future. For now, you will both stay here tonight - and you will both sleep! I must report to the council."

Old Bede smiled as he went out. Secretly he was tremendously proud of the two young mice and of Twitchwhisker especially. Not that he would admit to it. The last thing he wanted to do was encourage them further. He had enough grey hairs already!

The next morning Ezekiel, the council steward, entered Bede's chamber and told them some most welcome news. Reports had just reached the council that Morgana and Modred and others had been seen leaving the castle and what was more Wolfbane, in a wicker basket, was sighted going with them. Morgana was taking her terrible pet with her!

They all realized what that meant. With Wolfbane gone the mice of Camelot could look forward to much better pickings. Life would now be easier for the colony, for Wolfbane had been the greatest thorn in their side. It was true that Camelot was still home to other cats, as Bede had once observed there would always be cats in Camelot, but with Wolfbane's going the dangers they faced would never be as great again. And all this was due to the efforts of Twitchwhisker and Shortpaws.

Ezekiel turned to Twitchwhisker. "I have been asked by Amos to present his compliments to you on behalf of the council who request you and Shortpaws to attend them at the earliest opportunity."

"I wonder what they want?" Twitchwhisker asked Bede after Ezekiel's departure.

"I wonder," Bede said, smiling mysteriously. "Scut along now and make yourselves presentable. And try not to be too late."

"Late? Me late? Perish the thought," Twitchwhisker replied.

Shortly afterwards in the council chamber the two intrepid adventurers discovered why they had been summoned. Before all the mice of Camelot they were to be honoured. As a reward for his efforts it had been decided that Twitchwhisker would, from that moment onwards, be relieved of his general duties. He was assigned to the Supply Master's office and would learn from Bede all the skills required with a view that in the future should Bede retire or be unable to continue, he, Twitchwhisker, would be ready to take his place.

Amos expressed the council's fullest confidence in him and hoped that in return he would face his task to the best of his capabilities. Twitchwhisker was overcome with shock. He was stunned, left speechless for the first time in his life. Eventually he croaked his acceptance and promised he would do his utmost to deserve their confidence in him.

Shortpaws was not forgotten in all this. Henceforth he too would be relieved of general duties and be attached to the council to be trained as a steward.

Amos concluded the announcements by saying that in his humble opinion as long as the colony continued to produce mice such as Twitchwhisker and Shortpaws the future for Camelot mice was assured.

"Well, what do you have to say for yourself?" Bede asked when he found himself alone with Twitchwhisker.

"Whose idea was it?" asked Twitchwhisker.

Old Bede looked slyly at his young friend and new assistant. "The council's of course," Bede replied. "All important decisions are made by the council as you will discover when you become a member yourself. I must confess though that I did make one or two slight suggestions . . ."

"I thought you might have," Twitchwhisker said. "I didn't think you had such a high regard for me. Was it not you who called me irresponsible?"

"Ah, but much has happened since then," Bede said in his defence. "It may take some time to take off the rough edges but I believe that in the end you will buckle down to your responsibilities and be a credit to us all."

Twitchwhisker groaned dramatically. Bede had finally got the best of him. Before all Camelot mice he'd been honoured. Now he would have to change his ways.

"Don't look so dismayed," Bede offered brightly. "It isn't the end of the world."

"It's the end of adventuring though, isn't it," Twitchwhisker wailed in reply.

"I don't know about that," Bede observed with a twinkle in his wise old eyes. "A Supply Master must know every stone of the castle. I daresay you will be allowed time to explore from time to time as part of your duties."

Twitchwhisker brightened up considerably. Perhaps

118

things wouldn't be too bad after all.

"In fact," Bede continued, "I would like a report on preparations for tonight's feast. If you have nothing else to do at the moment I would greatly appreciate your observations."

Now it was the turn of Twitchwhisker's eyes to twinkle. "Actually I *am* free at the moment, Supply Master," he said. "And I would like to offer my services — that is if I can be spared?"

"I think I can manage for the time being," Bede replied, playing along with the game. "Try not to dawdle. I would like to have foraging plans ready as soon as possible."

"I shall be back before you can say 'bacon-rind'," Twitchwhisker said.

"Bacon-rind," Bede said.

But Twitchwhisker did not hear him. He was gone before the words were uttered.

Bede chuckled and shook his head. "Sometimes I wonder if I'm growing too old for all this," he said to himself and to the ancient stones of Camelot.